# THE BLUE KIND

THE BLUE

# KIND

*Kathryn Born*

SWITCHGRASS BOOKS    NORTHERN ILLINOIS UNIVERSITY PRESS    DeKalb

© 2012 by Switchgrass Books, an imprint of
Northern Illinois University Press
Published by the Northern Illinois University Press,
DeKalb, Illinois 60115
Manufactured in the United States using acid-free paper
All Rights Reserved
Design by Shaun Allshouse

This is a work of fiction. All characters are products of the author's imagination, and any resemblance to persons living or dead is entirely coincidental.

Library of Congress Cataloging-in-Publication Data

Born, Kathryn.
The blue kind / Kathryn Born.
p. cm.
Summary: "A dystopian drug—fantasy—brimming with a labyrinth plot and indelible characters—that unfold in the apocalyptic debris of an all but unrecognizable American city."— Provided by publisher.
ISBN 978-0-87580-682-2 (pbk.) —
ISBN 978-1-60909-067-8 (electronic)
I. Title.
PS3602.O763B58 2012
813'.6—dc23
2012030518

*This one is for Amy. And for Kaia.*

# THE BLUE KIND

The moment in
time before
everything went

blank

All is forgiven, and I return to the city we burned down long ago. In its current form, it's a metropolis called Neom, but hundreds of years ago it was a tiny village with a name I can't recall, and we spoke a language that's lost to me now. The single moment I can remember, the one unblurred thought, is standing on the mountain at dawn, overlooking a clump of village houses that sat quietly in the green dell below. The little houses were sweet and square, with shingled roofs nailed on by hand and doorways decorated with small rocks and flowers. I turned to look at Cory, with the distant clouds and gray walls of the West Mountains behind him, as his long arms pulled back the string of a bow that was almost as tall as his body. When he looked at me, I ignited the arrow, and it made a strange growling whisper as it sailed away into the silent morning. The first house burst into flames with a popping sound—we reloaded the bow and launched a stream of fiery arrows like a fast machine. It was a game, aiming at those little wood houses.

The fire spread from the houses to the trees, replaced their leaves with flames that shimmered and waved. A piece of flame dripped onto the meadow, and the fire spread, like small orange monsters clawing and crawling in every direction, racing through the grass and climbing up the mountain. The air was warm and filled with a cloud of smoke and the roar of burning things.

In that single moment, we felt like we had won, and we smiled at each other. We had taken our revenge, and it felt good to watch them pay for torturing us for so long. Cory's hair was even more orange in the light of the fire. He picked me up and spun me around. Like a child, I wrapped my legs around his waist and bent my head back, looking at the candy-coated blue sky and wondering if it would catch fire, too. I arched my back more to watch the spinning, upside-down world burn. The flames scaled the mountain and surrounded us, and it was all so beautiful.

As my train slows down into the cement underworld, I see Cory and Ray leaning against both sides of a thick support column. Ray is wearing his usual cowboy hat and sunglasses. Cory's hair is past his shoulders, and he's wearing big, baggy pants and a shirt that looks like it was cut from sackcloth. He takes his weight off the column and throws away his smoke. He seems to be looking right at me, but I know he can't see through the mirrored windows of the train that comes from Over. It's different from the other trains; the cars are dimly lit and no voice announces the station, no conductor pokes his head out from the train as it comes to a stop. The doors pull apart and I step out.

"Hi!" I squeal and throw my arms around Cory. I look up while we hug and see him craning his neck to peer into the train car, trying to get some clues about Over, about the place I come from. The train pulls away, and he finally looks down into my face.

"Hi, doll," he says and touches my hair. He seems shaky and excited.

Ray looks a little frayed, too, staring at his boots with his hands in his pockets. I turn and give him a big hug. He smiles and seems amazed to see me. "Hey, I know you!" he says. "I can't believe you're here. I just can't believe it. I had no idea you were coming." He takes off his cowboy hat and scratches his yellow hair, making it spike out like a dandelion while transitioning the conversation into silence. It seems weird that Cory hadn't told Ray I was coming back. I look to Cory for an explanation, but he just opens his mouth and closes it again. The train rumbles away and disappears down the tube. We start walking through a tunnel with long lights on the ceiling, spaced like lines on the highway. I wonder if it is day or night.

"So how are you?" I ask Cory.

"Good, how was Over?" He asks this casually, like I'm just going to blurt out an entire explanation for where I've been all this time. Instead I look at him and smile and nod my head.

"Over is over. It's nice to be back." I reach out and touch his twine necklace, which now holds a blocky indigo stone. "I see we've moved up a notch. What else is new in Neom?"

"Not a thing. Everyone in our neighborhood is still really high, and the laws of physics are just as lax as before." He reaches into one of his many pockets and offers me my old wedding bracelet. "You left this behind."

"Hey! You kept it for me!" I feel a little sheepish, and say lightly, "Guess I was in a bit of a rush getting out of here last time." I give Cory a goofy smile while I balance on one foot and snap the wedding band around my ankle.

Ray looks up, pops back into the conversation. "Nice to see you. What was your name again?"

"Funny, Ray."

"You're not going to tell me?" he asks in a low, flat voice.

"Tell you what?"

"Your name."

Ray is not smiling. I see myself confused and stretched wide in the reflection of his sunglasses. I take them off his face and see in his glassy blue eyes that he doesn't remember my name. He looks away, sniffs, and looks back at me. He says, "I'm sorry. My memory isn't the best."

I hope this is a joke. "My name is Alison, but everyone calls me Alley," I say and shake his hand.

"Ray. Glad to meet you." He is not joking.

Cory is glazed and unhelpful. This is all a little awkward. "Well," I say, "let's go up into the light."

"They've really changed a lot of things while you've been gone," Cory says, making conversation to break the strange vibe. "See, look: electric stairs." Cory steps on first, then me, then Ray. Cory rises up, turns and bends down to kiss me. The stairs carry us up into the bright sunlight, and it feels like a warm spring day.

On the street, we stand out like rainbow ragamuffins among the businesspeople who scurry to and fro. They are wearing khaki and white, walking with a purposeful and un-intoxicated gait. They have a certainty that they are heading somewhere, a certainty I do not share.

We head out from the center of the city, walking down rows of tall and smooth buildings. Some are covered with mirrors that break the sky into a grid of disjointed cloud squares. The cars look like bars of soap. The sky seems dirti-er, and the sun seems farther away. I don't say anything when I notice Cory's shadow getting out of step with Cory, but then the foot of his shadow peels off the sidewalk and Cory trips over it. Cory quickly stands up as if nothing happened, and Ray keeps on walking, oblivious. I hold Cory back and let Ray get out of earshot.

"What's wrong with Ray?"

"What do you mean?"

"He doesn't remember my name."

"Ray doesn't remember anything. Wasn't he like that when you left?"

"No. I don't think so."

"Hmmm. Well, it must've happened after you left."

I look at Ray moving farther away from us. "Won't he get lost?"

"Nah, he knows his way home."

"Oh." We start to walk again.

"He remembers some stuff," Cory says. "I knew you were coming today when this bubble floated in front of me, com-pletely out of nowhere. And it just hung in front of my face, even in the wind. Then it popped, and I said to Ray, 'We need to get Alison.' And he didn't know who you were at first, but then I told him about your long brown hair, your big brown eyes"—he smiles at me—"your tan-colored skin and your big boobs, and Ray goes, 'She's been gone a long time?' and I was like, 'Yeah, that's right.' Then he said that he missed you. So he's got the important stuff right."

"Then how come he doesn't know my name?"

"That's just the way Ray is now. Every time he gets lit, he starts over. He'll stare into space and the memories unravel. And it's all gone, just like that." He does a snap with his fingers that makes his lighter flip open and spark a flame.

I don't say anything. He looks at me while he lights his cocosmoke. "It's not so bad," he says, shrugging it off like it's not a big deal.

"Maybe it's old age. Maybe we're finally starting to get sick."

"Maybe."

"Maybe we'll get it, too."

"Maybe."

"So he doesn't remember anything that happened? A thousand years of memories are just gone?"

"I don't know, Alley. I don't know what he knows."

He flops his arm around my shoulders, and I put my arm around his waist. We resume the formation we've walked in for as long as I can remember.

"It's not the end of the world," he says. "I mean, when it gets right down to it, what is there to remember, anyway?"

We leave the busy center of Neom and keep walking outward, passing through Runaway Village, crowded with a new batch of kids. The ones who were around last time have grown up and moved on, but we still blend right in with the teenagers. As we pass rows of quaint, short-stack apartments, I start trying to guess which one will be ours, but we keep walking, keep passing through until the neighborhood grows strangely quiet. As we travel, more abandoned houses and decrepit factories appear. A car passes us, and we all look at each other, like it's odd to see anyone in this ghost town. Paper bags get caught by the wind and roll down the street like tumbleweeds.

We catch up with Ray, who is leaning against the wooden facade of an old-fashioned theater. It stands about four stories high, and all the windows are boarded up. Painted in faint blue-gray letters is a sign: *The Never Netherland Theatre.*

"Well, this is it," Cory says.

"This is what?"

"This is where we live. We're squatting."

"Really?"

"Hey, c'mon. It's really cool inside. And there's no rent. Ray will show you around, and you can move your stuff in."

"I don't have anything."

"Oh, okay. Come up to the roof when you're done; I have a surprise for you." He kisses me, walks backward a couple of steps, and says, "Have Ray show you the stars he made."

Ray and I look at each other.

"Do you want to show me around?" I ask.

"Sure. Show you around where?"

Ray holds his butane lighter above his head like a torch as he shows me the auditorium. Ray is smiling because he is always smiling—his lips are just shaped that way. It is a massive room, with three blocks of seats and two aisles. Above and behind us are balcony seats. The side walls have box seats, and above our heads, stars glow in the ceiling as little spots of light.

"Did you make those?" I ask.

"Did I?"

I pause, then try a different question. "Hey, Ray, if you wanted to make a star, what would you do?"

"I would catch some light in a box and pour it into the sky."

There is something lonely about Ray without his memory. Something is missing, something loving and friendly. Our shared history has evaporated, and I realize that beyond memories, the thing that is missing from Ray . . . is me.

"Ray?"

"Ow," he says, and the lighter goes out. I think it burned his fingers. It is pitch black now. "Yes?" he says, out of the dark.

"Do you know who I am?"

"I don't know." I hear him sniff. "Do you know who I am?"

The tour continues. We go into the theater lobby where light seeps in through the boarded windows. Ray opens a door to a pitch-black room. A stairway descends into black water after a few steps. We stand in the doorway of something so vast and empty, it's like stairs that end at the beginning of the universe. As we gaze into the abyss, a sudden realization grips my lungs. I hold on to the doorframe, suddenly frightened of falling in.

"Is this water from the flood?" I look at Ray as he stares blankly at the water. I square his shoulders to face me. "Ray, don't you remember the flood? When you carried me over the river?"

He shakes his head and looks sad.

"Terrible things happened after the flood, and you had to carry me home. You don't know anything about this?" I shake my head, and my voice rises. "You don't remember?"

Ray shuts the door and says, "Let's move on."

I don't feel like moving on, but I put one foot in front of another and we go up the stairs to a projection booth. It looks like somebody lives in this tiny room. There is a terra-cotta pot with a single rose, a corner area with a pillow and blankets, and a glass cage containing a motionless brown snake as big as a scarf. I am immediately haunted; I hate snakes.

We go upstairs, past the balcony seats, into a big, dark attic with a slanted ceiling. The walls meet together above our heads, and the room is shaped like a long prism. The front wall is boarded up, and the back wall is covered with a rainbow tie-dyed tapestry. A stop sign on top of a box serves as a table for ashtrays and small crap. There are mats and blankets on the floor.

"This is a room," Ray says.

"This is our room?"

"Uhhh." He turns around in a circle. "I think so."

"Oh."

"Hey, what was your name again?"

"Alison."

"Hey, Alison, welcome home."

"Thanks." And my eyes well up with tears.

We climb the fire escape all the way up to the roof of the theater. Cory is waiting for us, with some food cooking on a little grill. There are three chairs, and we sit together under the setting sun, the purple layer of the sky above the strips of blue and orange, and the sun sitting at the bottom, underlined by a thin pink line. Cory gives me a box, and inside it is something made out of red paper, tied with red string.

"Do you want to see how it works?"

I nod. He pulls the red string, and it begins to open; it's a paper flower as delicate as a butterfly's skeleton. It's beautiful. He pulls until it fully blooms.

"Okay, now smell it."

I put my face inside the petals of the flower, and Cory gives the string one final tug. The center pops open and releases a burst of red pollen that I inhale in surprise. Cory is smiling. "This is Oxo. It's pretty Zen; it'll keep you from taking things seriously."

It kicks in. "Right on," I say, sticking my whole head in the flower and inhaling what's left. "I'm going to need it to kill the sadness of being homeless."

"Hey, staying in the theater is free, and you get what you pay for, ark ark." Cory wads up the pollen-dusted paper from the center of the flower and pops it into his mouth.

We sit on the roof in the perfect weather, feeling like the teenagers we appear to be on the outside. We make fun of the problems that come with being eternally stuck in the awkwardness of adolescence. Ray has chronic acne and boners, I don't understand why sex is a big deal, and Cory has a voice that randomly shoots up an octave. We're screwed.

But we laugh as the boys tell a story about how Ray lost his arm in a train accident. Standing on the roof in the setting sun, they pantomime the tale. Cory plays the role of Ray, first chasing down his foot, which was stuck in the train's axle. As he tries to pull his foot out of the spinning wheels, his hand gets caught and it pulls off his arm! With some prompting, Ray acts out Cory chasing after him, carrying his lost arm and shouting to him. They finish with the triumphant end—Ray growing a new foot and his severed arm snapping back on "like two magnets coming together and sticking."

It's important to be able to laugh about things like that.

Cory has missed me, and his attention feels like the warm sun shining on my face. It feels so good to be back with Cory that I can push aside the fact that things have gone even farther downhill. I remind myself that all is forgiven and let Cory's arm around my shoulder give the same protection it always used to provide. He keeps looking at me and smiling; he tenderly puts my hair behind my ear and kisses my cheek as he holds me close.

"I'm so glad you're home," he keeps saying.

Some of it
wasn't very nice,
but most of it
was beautiful

I am awake.

I am alone. I do not know where I am.

I am not in Over. I am in Neom. I came back yesterday.

As my eyes adjust to the dark, and my brain gets used to the headache, the previous night comes back to me. After our barbecue on the roof, Cory and I set up blankets and unrolled thick sleeping mats in the box seats of the theater. We slept together, and slept together some more, his body hard and familiar.

He must have left when I was sleeping.

I try to navigate by the light of Ray's stars above, grope around for the low wall of the box seats, and finally knock into it. This half circle is like a little balcony that overlooks the auditorium, and Ray's stars glow above. One is dimmer than all the others. I wonder what will happen to it. My stomach feels a pang of worry. I finally find the curtain door, and in the upper lobby there's enough sunlight coming in through the edges of the boarded windows to make my way to the attic. The room is as hot as a bread oven.

Since the two side walls lean together to make a ceiling, I can stand upright in the middle and move a few steps to each side before my head touches the slanted ceiling. The front and back walls are triangles, and light seeps through the edges of the front window that's boarded up with a flat square of wood. I decide that I am not going to live in a dark room and start prying the nails off with a nail I found on the floor. Prying nails with other nails takes forever, and I wish I had a hammer. I remove enough of them to pull the edge of the board away from the wall. My fingers are killing me, but I yank and wrestle, sweat and swear, until, with one last good pull, the final nail squeaks and the board falls away, revealing a perfectly round hole almost big enough to stand in.

The wind gushes in, and it is an amazing view. I didn't realize how high we were. The attic is flooded with sunlight and cool, fresh air. A stoplight below turns green, but nothing moves. There are some abandoned buildings across the street, and ghostly buildings in the distance have grown so tall they scrape the sky. Over to the side , there is an empty space where I can see past the city to the factories that pump dark gray clouds from silver pipes. In another area, a water tank stands like a white metal moon on a stick, hovering over the buildings.

I sit with my legs dangling out the circle, watching the world stand still. It is very quiet here in the ghost-town section of Neom, and maybe the space and quiet are a good thing, maybe the elevation will give us some perspective. Neom always looks better from a distance, anyway. So I sit and watch the streetlight change color, thinking about last night when Cory and I were together, in the box seats, lying naked on blankets with a lit candle between us. We were glad to be back together; we smiled and gazed at each other like we were new to each other's eyes. I was thinking what a beauty he is, and how he's my opposite. I'm all circles—big brown eyes, a round face, and curvy—and Cory is one of those tall, skinny dudes who looks like a skeleton when you're on hallucinogens. He has wide, green cat eyes and high cheekbones, a perfectly sculpted triangular face with sharp teeth.

Whenever I first come back to town, there's always an awkward moment when Cory and I size each other up, sniff around for changes. And in those first moments, there does seem to be a glaze of change that coats us. But away from the light of the world, and with our bodies touching, all the differences melt away and it's just Cory and me again. The past is forgiven, and we come together like we've always been, for as long as I can remember. We're two statues that have rusted in the rain and become soldered together as one.

So in the half circle of the box seats, we talked into the night. Cory was propped on one elbow, giving me updates.

"Everyone still gets high. The Neom city squares do it so they can keep working nonstop, and the hipsters in Runaway Village do it so they won't work at all. Same as always. And all through Neom, the laws of physics are still pretty lax, but I've moved up a level. I used to be a peddler, see, but now I'm a mover, and our rank has moved up a notch."

"But it's still selling drugs," I said.

"No, drugs are gone."

"What?"

"Nope, no drugs, just mugs, like the red flower last night. They're a new breed of intoxicants, and they've wiped out the old ones. Alcohol is gone now; it's been replaced with Cloud 9, which is a cleaner version. You missed it, Alley. They called it The Golden Age of Pharmaceuticals, and it happened right after scientists discovered how to isolate parts of the brain to the point where they could make mugs with incredibly specific effects. So they could create a drug that only affects your mental relationship with gravity and makes you feel like you're floating. They could make mugs that let you assemble objects faster, or create an emotional block to keep your personal demons at bay. So suddenly there are a whole bunch of new mugs, the Feudal Government says they're good for you, and they're all legal."

"Did you go out of business?"

He laughed. "No, that's what everybody thought would happen, but it's always more complicated than that. On top of everything, the science wasn't perfect, and the Feudals got involved by making mandates about who should do what mugs, and really fucking things up. As time went on, things start going wrong with the mugs: people don't just feel like they're floating, they actually start floating away; some people get trapped in nightmares; all sorts of bizarre stuff. And the biggest problem—I mean, not for us, being mug dealers and all—is that they get addicted despite the claim that the new mugs are not supposed to be habit-forming." Cory found his box of cocosmokes and lit one. "So the Feudals start losing their heads, demanding the scientists design a new batch to correct the problems. That doesn't work. Then they start adding laws. Some mugs become illegal, and they create a whole nonsensical system of degrees ranging from mugs they call 'recommended' to mugs they label 'banned.' Once some mugs become illegal, people start hoarding legal mugs in case their status changes. Then mug formulas hit the streets, and there's an instantaneous black market."

"And that's where we come in," I said.

"Yup. I mean, everyone is high now; it's in the air. The mugs that make you work fast for long periods of time stay legal. The ones that let you live in a dream, well, they'll toss you in jail for those. But the real problem is that they're making new mugs all the time, the big companies right along with people cooking it up in labs in their basements. Nobody even knows what the hell they're selling, let alone what they're taking."

"Sounds like a mess," I said and lay back down on the blankets. I looked at the stars and felt a strange sense of déjà vu. "I thought drugs were just fine the way they were."

"Well, everything changes. Hey, speaking of mugs—" Cory said, reaching for his pants and pulling containers out of the pockets. His pants were incredibly baggy with dozens of pockets, the fashion equivalent of a briefcase filled with mugs.

"Where is Atom in all this?" I asked, and Cory froze.

"He made a fortune," Cory said without looking up.

"Goddamnit," I said softly, snatching a blanket and standing up, covering myself. I put my elbows on the rim of the box seats and looked at Ray's stars. The warm intimate moment was gone, and we didn't say anything for a long time. Cory lay silently on the floor. I took a deep breath and finally said, "So he's still Kingpin."

"Yes."

"And I'm still a chain?"

"Alley—"

I put my dress back on. "What am I supposed to say? That it's cool to be in the same mess as before? That it's cool to be human collateral if a deal goes bad?" Cory doesn't move or say anything. "We have to get out of here, Cory. We have to leave Neom."

"Alley!" Cory's voice cracked. "I don't deal with Atom. I promised before and I kept my promise. Everything is different now, things are safer, the supply is more stable. We have a real chance of making a killing and cashing out."

"Atom's a fucking monster."

"Alley, I promise." More silence. Then, out of the quiet, out of the dark, he said, "I'm sorry about what happened last time."

My throat tightened and my eyes filled with tears. "You're sorry? That's your apology for selling me down the river? Your apology for giving me to another man?" Tears fell, and I wiped them away with the hem of my dress. I sat back on the floor with the candle between us. "You promise me, Cory, you promise me right now that things will be different this time."

"I promise."

"I'm your wife, Cory. I'll run around and act like your disposable teenage girlfriend for the sake of the business, but never forget that I am your wife, and have been your wife for five hundred years. We'll do what's necessary until we can get out of these dire straits, but never forget that we're just pretending to be a part of this system. Alright?"

"Alright," he said, and we held each other in the dark until we fell asleep.

Now, in the light of day, looking at the skyline, I notice something different about the world. The sky has an aching stretch of loneliness to it. The blue dome looks overgrown, or like it's too far away. Maybe it's me that's different, and Neom is just the same. I look out the window now and try to put my finger on what has changed in the landscape. It's more than just a feeling; something is missing in the lone stretch of sky, where the clouds are torn and piled on each other.

And I realize in a flash that the mountains are gone.

*peace pot microdot*
*Jesus loves you wasted or not*

I am frantic when Cory comes home.

"Wow. Cool hole in the wall," he says, stumbling a step backward. His head is tilted to the side like a wilting orange flower, petals flopped down.

"Cory? Honey?"

"Yes, doll?"

"Ah, where are the mountains?"

"What mountains?"

"The mountains that used to be over there?" I point.

"Ummm," he slurs. "Wow. Okay. Alley, the mountains have been gone a really, really long time, like, a hundred years or something." He is teetering and swaying, holding a smoke.

"Where did they go?"

"They . . . fucking . . . blew them up and bulldozed them." He peers at me, his eyes glazed. "Alley, don't look so surprised. They've been gone a long time. They were gone last time you came back from Over, and I think the time before that, when you came back from Over"—he messily waves

his cigarette hand to indicate the chopped pieces of time—
"maybe the time before that, before you took off . . . again.
'Member? They knocked them down because they had to
build something . . ." He holds out his hands. "Big."

He leans against the wall and slides down until he's sitting. I
go over and sit next to him. He reaches into one of his pockets
and takes out a pack of gum labeled Atlantos and offers me
a stick. We stare out the new window in silence as I try to
remember the mountains being demolished. The only sound
is me chewing the wad of gum that's becoming increasingly
difficult to chew. When I try to turn my head to look at Cory
and ask more questions about the mountains, it takes a very
long time, as if I'm immersed in thick syrup.

"How's that gum treating you?" Cory asks, with a slow
wicked smile, and pops a piece in his mouth.

My eyes get wide, very slowly, and I smile very slowly and try
to ask, "What's in the gum?" All that comes out is the longest
version of the word "dude" I've ever spoken. It comes out funny
and I try to laugh, but it comes out, "Ha." Big silence. "Ha."

Then Cory starts to laugh, and it comes out the same way.
We are laughing hysterically, like morons in slow motion.
Our long ha-ha-has float through the syrupy air, across the
room, and hit the wall with a soft "ha" sound.

This is idiotic, but it's awesome. We get up and try to dance
around, pushing our hands and legs through the thick air. I
kick one leg up and it stays up there, so I try to kick it with
my other foot. But with both feet in the air, I am not standing
on anything, so I slowly fall to the floor.

"It didn't
hurt
to fall," I say.
"Be

careful." Cory reaches out with one finger and touches my nose.

"It will
hurt
later."

When Ray comes back up, we are still dancing in slow motion. Cory gives him a stick of gum, and soon Ray is calling out, "Hey diddle diddle," and hearing it ricochet off the walls.

The sun sinks down and comes by the circle window. It leaves a nice oval of yellow light that slowly slides back toward the other end of the room. Ray gets up and carefully lays an open shoe box on its side, facing the window. Then he sits back down, and we watch the setting sun's oval light slide into the box and fill it with light. Ray puts the cover on and traps the sunlight inside the shoe box. We hear the light splashing around.

Ray says,
"Got it.
Come on."

We waddle down the attic stairs and crawl out on the catwalk above the sky of the theater. Ray reaches through the grate to the sky of the auditorium and unscrews the cap. Inside it has a fixture for a light bulb in a glass bowl. He pours the light from the box, and it obediently falls like sand, filling the bowl with a glowing light. He recaps the star.

"Deuuuude," is all I say. I used to wonder where the stars came from.

Now I know.

Walking back to the attic, my heart starts to race out of control, and I begin to shake. "Cory, my heart."

He hands me another stick of gum. I feel better as we get to the attic. We play a game where we take guesses about what's inside the box chest that serves as the base to our stop sign table. It is hard to talk. The boys' voices seem so low, a record player slowing down.

"Maybe

an

ocean,

yeah?" Ray says and tilts his head. Then he freezes in space, and I hear his words echo. Their talk is muffled, and Ray's image is frozen, his head cocked and his yellow hair sticking out in all directions. I do not understand this. I try to reach out, but I can't move my arms. I can't move my mouth, I cannot breathe, and my heart is not beating.

I hear muffled yelling. They are shaking my body very hard, but the frozen image of Ray doesn't move. Something hits my head with a whack. The image of Ray looking at me with his head tilted is shattered into blackness. My heart starts to beat.

"Alley, c'mon, c'mon, come around!" Cory is yelling. Then I start to see him, like the lights slowly turning back on. The boys are peering into my face, looking worried. I scream because I am so freaked out by what just happened, and because I couldn't scream before. Cory hugs me, and we rock together in a slow, steady rhythm until I am breathing right and my heart slows down.

"It's okay, you're alright, your system's just not used to it." I hold on tight while he keeps rocking me. Ray squats beside us and pets my hair.

"If I were a normal person, would I have died?" I ask.

"If we were normal people, we would've paid better attention to how many sticks we were chewing."

I sober up and calm down while the boys chew more At-
lantoses. I am wiped out and my body aches. I arrange the
sleeping mats and blankets for Cory and myself. Ray likes to
sleep on the pile of cushions. I lie on the mat, stare through
the circle window to the street-lit sky, feeling like it's on me
to make our lives work this time, to build something strong
enough so the wind won't blow it all away. So Atom won't
strike again. So the Workers from Over can't just bust in and
haul me out of here.

Eventually Cory finishes his last smoke and hobbles like
an old man over to our mat. We curl up like spoons.

"So the mountains have been gone a long time?" I ask
Cory.

"Uh-huh," he says slowly.

"It seems like they were just here yesterday."

"Well
for us
yesterday was
a
long
time
ago."

It feels good to have Cory's hand on my breast, and warm
to feel his breathing on my neck. We fall asleep this way.

"Hey."

"Hmmm. Mmmm," I say and swat away Cory's attempt to shake me awake.

"You wanted me to wake you when I got up. So I'm trying to wake you, but I think you want to stay asleep," Cory says.

"Mmmm."

"I gotta do a bunch of stuff. I'll be back around dark."

Sitting up but still asleep, I wrap my arms around him and pull him back down on the mat with me. "Stay stay stay," I say.

We lie together, and he curls up with me for a bit afterward, but then he wants to go. Once Cory is awake, he likes to get right up. Me, I could sleep all day.

"I need money," I say.

"I know. And yes, there are mugs around for you and Ray to play with."

Later I wake up sweaty and with a headache; the attic smells like tar. I don't know how Ray sleeps through this heat. Beside me is a line of little jars and boxes and a pack of currency. I grab the coins and go to the Easy Store down the street. Our neighborhood is deserted, but still there is an Easy Store close by. How is this possible? Are they everywhere, or are all the other empty buildings filled with mice like us? I buy the supplies that I need to clean myself and the attic. They barely make a dent in the big wad of currency. Cory must be doing pretty well.

At home I pour the expensive powder into the expensive bucket, add water, and start scrubbing the floor like a woman possessed. Cory doesn't intentionally ash on the floor, but the table is a disgrace; it's just a stop sign on top of a box, and it tips over many times a day, along with all the bottles and ashtrays. I scrub on my hands and knees, getting rid of the sticky filth that coats the floor. When the whole surface is done except where Ray is sleeping, I wake him up, make him move. He goes to the long round hole in the wall and sits on the edge with his legs hanging out.

There is a knock at the bottom of the stairs. My blood rushes to my head, preparing for the horror that anyone knocking will surely bring.

"Hello?" It is a girl's voice. I go to the stairs and look down.

She is a broom of a girl, with wheat-colored hair down to her waist. We are both wearing long dresses. She has a round face and round blue eyes. I think we look like photo negatives of each other, except she looks pretty nervous and I bet I look pretty mad.

"What?" I say, trying to keep my tone of voice steady, despite my adrenaline.

"Oh," she says. "Is Cory here?"

"No," I say and take a step down the stairs toward her.

"My name's Dilly Dally." She takes a step back with every step I go down. "I used to be called Cory, too, but then I changed it because it would be too confusing. Cory and Cory, see? Isn't that funny?"

"No, it's not."

Her smile melts like snow and falls off her face.

"Tell Cory I stopped by," she says, her voice much lower and with less breath. Her friendly bit is over. Both our bodies are having an internal flight-or-fight debate.

"No, I won't tell him."

"Why?" Her hands are shaking.

"Because this isn't your place anymore, and you shouldn't be here."

"Look, it's got nothing to do with you, it's just a chain thing. When you're not here, he's going to find somebody else." She looks past me and smiles suddenly. "Hey, Ray, I'll find you in the park later, okay?" She is all sunshine and roses now. I turn and look at Ray, who nods his head like a stupid child.

She looks at me again. "Well, it was nice to meet you . . ."

"Alison."

"Alison."

She leaves, and I hear her footsteps fading into the distance.

"Who was that girl, Ray?"

"I don't know," he says, not taking his eyes off the place where Dilly Dally stood.

"Has she been around here before?" I am shrieking.

"I don't remember."

"Jesus, Ray, don't you remember anything? You don't remember if she lived here? If she slept where I sleep?"

I go back to my scrubbing, under my breath mocking her line about how when I'm not here, Cory is going to find someone else. Ray wanders around, trying to stay out of my way. I finish the floor violently. I look at the stop sign on the table and won't make any more guesses about what is inside the box. I take the sign off, lift the cover, and see that it's filled with junk, except for my old tri-knife, which I hold in my hand with the blades poking out between each finger.

I put the knife in my pocket and start looking at the line of mugs.

Each little jar and box has a glossy label with the name of the mug and a little advertisement for it. We pick two containers and hope they mix alright. The jar of Sart has a label in muted pastels and flowing writing that says, "Need a break? Go outside . . . of yourself." Chill Pillz advertises, "Beat the heat, be cool and chill." We double the recommended dose and otherwise follow the instructions, gobbling Chill Pillz and putting drops of Sart on the insides of our wrists, then rubbing them together like putting on perfume.

I don't know which mug kicks in first. My head gets the nice feeling of being wrapped up in cool cotton. Then something in me stands still, and the fire that was burning through my veins over that stupid girl is cooled and soothed. This is good, this is alright. I think of Dilly Dally, and there is no flash of hot lightning. I look at Ray and smile with my mouth closed.

"How do you feel?"

"Right on," he says, and we decide to walk to Runaway Village and go dress shopping, since my old dress has faded to gray and is too warm for this season. The Village has the same cotton dresses from last time, with long skirts comfortable enough to sleep in, as most of them are pretty shapeless and saggy. Since we've moved up to blue rank and I've got a big wad of currency, I want something better. We find the only store that sells new clothes, and I see a white dress that has a fitted bodice top with a built-in bra and thin little straps. The long skirt flows, and it hides my big butt. I like it, it's cleavage-intensive. I will dye it blue myself. I spend a lot of money on it since it is, after all, my uniform and I'll wear it almost every day. I get some high black summer boots made of lightweight cloth that I saw the girls in the park wearing.

I like this dress white, and it makes me sad to imagine it some faded shade of blue. It would be nice to live in a place where I could wear any color dress I wanted. When the girl behind the counter asks, "Just the dress?" and doesn't try to chitchat, I realize that it's a new generation and no one knows I'm a chain yet. So for today, for one day, I will wear it white and not be the kind of girl who has to wear a color uniform to show her Jack's rank in the mug world.

At least I don't have to dye it orange; those girls have it bad, and the chains in red are practically homeless. Wait, come to think of it, *we're* practically homeless. I change into my new dress and find Ray in a back room with hats on pegs all over the walls. I ask him how he likes my dress. He reaches with both hands for my breasts.

"No," I say and slap his hands away.

"No?"

"No."

We look at all the hats, and I feel kind of mean and curious about this memory-loss thing, feel like testing it. I reach over and take off Ray's cowboy hat, and we try on new ones, looking in the mirror. While he's wearing a different cowboy hat,

I distract him, hang his hat on a hook, and move toward the door. But some bell goes off in Ray's head; he stops still and just stands, looking very intently at a spot on the floor, like he's looking at a bug from another planet. He says, "Something is wrong."

"Well, whatever, let's go."

"Nope. Can't leave. Something is wrong." He walks around the hat room.

I start to hassle him. "C'mon, Ray, I don't care. Let's go."

He gets close to me with his glassy eyes, narrows them a little, and says, "I don't care, either." I realize now that Sart makes you numb not just to your own problems, but everyone else's.

He walks around in circles, finally catching himself in the mirror with the wrong cowboy hat on his head. "Where's my hat?" he says, and then sees it on the wall. He points at it and laughs, puts it on his head, and is ready to go. He says if it was a snake, it would've bit him.

We decide to get food and have a picnic on Cricket Hill.

"It's by where we used to live. I think I could still find it," I say.

We get on the train above ground and sit facing the back, which is an odd feeling, seeing the world only after it's passed you by, stretching away like taffy. With a head full of Sart, I don't have to feel things too strongly, can see things as they are and not the way I so badly want them to be.

I recognize our stop, and we climb up Cricket Hill. Now with the mountains gone, this is the only elevated spot remaining; the rest of Neom is completely flat. We stand at the top, where we can see everything. For me and the boys, getting some distance from the world became a strange necessity, a bond that tied us together. When we would get lost from one another, we would climb to the highest peak and find the others there. Now we are mountain people with no mountain. Unable to get high from height, trying to get high in other ways.

We eat and then lie on our backs with our hands for pillows. The sun shines on our heads. Ray looks at me with one eye closed.

"Alison," I say.

"Thank you," he says. "I was wondering." His hair sprawls on the grass like a dandelion. Ray is a husky, sturdy-looking dude, and you can see the muscles in his legs when he crosses one ankle over his knee. We watch the clouds fly over us, their soft underbellies gray. "You know," he says, "I don't remember a damn thing. I don't know anything about you, or where you're from, but I know we're close and I know I can trust you. I know that when I get confused, you're the one I can ask."

"Well, thanks, Ray. That's a nice thing to say. Do you have any questions you want to ask?"

"Are you my wife?"

"No. I'm Cory's wife."

"Nope." He shakes his head against the grass. "You feel like my wife, and I'm never wrong with what I feel. Can't remember a damn thing, but always trust my gut feeling."

I explain that his wife was Nikki and that she left when we came down from the mountains, and he lives with us now.

Ray gives me a sly look, shakes his head again. "Nope. My brain might be jelly, but no man with a wife who looks like you is going to have her living in a one-room attic with another man, going on picnics, and lying down on hilltops. Trust me, I'm your husband."

I shake my hand and wave the whole discussion away. But secretly I realize he's got a point. Cory's not the crazy-jealous type, but he has his territorial moments. I become defensive.

"You had a wife, Ray, and she was a good woman. But she had no tolerance for all this nonsense with the ball-and-chain collateral system. I love Cory and was willing to compromise, but Nikki would have no part of it. We lived in hiding in the mountains for many years, and when we finally came back down, she just kept walking. So I'm sorry, Ray, but I'm not Nikki; I'm her friend Alison."

"Women change names, just like cities change names. A man knows his wife."

"Well, I know who I am, and I know who Nikki was." I prop myself up on one elbow, to better argue. "We were different—I'm loose, I'm cool with living in a bizarre drug-trade system and squatting in the outskirts of Runaway Village. We all like it there because the laws of physics are more lax than in the rest of Neom, and the mugs kick ass. So add it all together and the place can be either magical or horrific—depends on the day. We're doing about the best we can, considering we're stuck being immortal and we have to kill the time somehow."

Ray is quiet, and his eyes look up to one side of the sky and then the other while he takes it all in. "I can't even begin to think about where to ask questions," he says.

I flop back down on the grass.

"Oh, Ray, even if you could understand it, it still wouldn't make sense. Trust me on that one. You know, we were all here when the ball-and-chain system was getting started. It was after Drug War II broke out, and all the soldiers became dealers when the war ended. Cory got swept up in all that. The problem is that no Jack has the money to pay for the mugs up front, so there has to be collateral. And since the men had done the dying during the war, the women were willing to sacrifice themselves to make peace. And getting traded for drugs was always just supposed to be ceremonial, just a symbol to show you were serious about repaying the debt. But then the Poetic Justice system became completely corrupt, and a dealer named Atom came into power, and he and Cory made a deal that went bad, and . . ."

My throat gets tight, and I can't go on with the story; even on Sart it's still too sad.

Ray tries to help. "Things got so ugly it would make a train take a dirt road?"

I look over at Ray and smile. "Yes. And I got traded to the Kingpin. And then I was given back to Cory. Now we're hiding in the theater so we need less currency and can be independent from Atom. But we've always been hiding, anyway, because whenever people get wind that we're immortal, they feel the need to give killing us a fair shake."

We watch the clouds.

I say, "Ray, I was hoping things would be different this time, but I'm getting a vibe that it's worse. With all these new mugs, there are more ways for it to go wrong. Even Cory had to admit that the chain system is in the center of it all—the better your chain is, or the more chain links you have, the better fronts you can get. The top suppliers will take bigger chances with you, hoping you screw up.

"In the old days, all the chains were wives and girlfriends. Now the girls in the chain system don't seem to care who they're chained to, so for them it's no big deal if they get traded; they're just junkies, just mug whores." I stop talking and look at the sky. I think of the girl with the wheat-colored hair, and it does not hurt. The cotton ball softness is going through my skin.

"Why can't I remember anything?"

"I'm not sure, Ray. These new mugs are strong, and there are public health posters all over the place about Mushy Brain Syndrome from doing too many mugs. Cory says it's Feudal propaganda, but who the fuck knows."

It is quiet.

"There's a monster," he says.

"Where?"

"See, with his mouth open."

"Oh, I see it. A dolphin, with a gray stomach." The sky is purple, and the clouds glow pink and fluffy. There are things in the clouds that do not have names but still could be real, someday, somewhere, just not here. We get quieter and quieter, and then we fall asleep.

Dilly Dally's words echo in my head. *When you're not here, he's going to find somebody else.* We wake up, let down by the mugs. A panicky feeling crawls all over me.

I shake Ray. "We gotta go, man, we gotta go right now."

Ray snaps awake, jumps to his feet, suddenly in the same panic I'm in. "Goddamn what?" he barks, and it startles the hell out of me and I say, shaky, "It's okay, it's alright; we took mugs to make us numb, and now it all wore off. There's got to be something at home to make this kickback softer."

Goddamn, I am mad about that girl. Here I was thinking he was doing errands. I wonder how many times Dilly Dally was on the list of things to do. I'm burning so mad,

I walk faster and faster. Ray seems quiet and freaked out, and he probably doesn't know why. Cory is gonna get the surprise of his life when he comes home. It would be good to spring out from behind something and attack, or better yet, throw something from the window and nail him before he steps in the door.

As we head up Brogan Avenue, I reach into my pocket and hold my tri-knife in my palm, trying not to squeeze the blades. In the attic, Cory is lying on the floor, with his ankle resting on his knee, balancing the hilt of his sword on the palm of his hand. The point sways in the air as Cory moves his hand slightly to keep it straight up.

I whip my tri-knife at him, and it spins as it heads right for his face. But Cory is suddenly on the ball; he catches his sword hilt in his hand and knocks the knife out of the air. It falls to the floor as I grab the stop sign and throw it like a Frisbee so it will cut off his head. Cory was starting to stand, but ducks, and the sign flies out the window. I look for something else to throw, but he grabs me and I punch him in the face real hard. He hooks his leg around my ankles, pulls my feet out from under me, and there I am, pinned to the floor.

"Get off me!" I scream in his ear.

"What?" he yells, panting.

"That girl, Dilly Dally." I remain pinned while he weighs his options.

"Fine. Okay," he says and rolls off. "C'mon, Alison. It's nothing and you know it."

"Don't give me that bullshit!" I yell, and then yell a whole bunch more. I'm in full-blown rant mode, and I'm rolling like a steam train. Every other woman he's had, since the history of time, is coming back to me clear as a goddamn

bell—I'm like a fucking savant with a pinpointed histori-
cal timeline of all his trespasses. And the entirety of it is
going to get dealt with right now, while I'm real lit and on
a roll. Cory responds to each new name by throwing back
his head and groaning.

Even I get tired of it after a while. Finally I ask, "Why do
you always have to find someone when I'm gone? Why can't
you just wait for me?"

"Because you go away for really long jags of time. That's
why. And what about you? Do you have some guy in Over,
waiting for you to come back?"

"No," I snap, but when honesty sets in, I add, "Not anymore." We both look down at the floor and don't say anything for a very long time.

Finally Cory says, "Okay, then. Fair is fair. No more acting
like a fucking angel."

After a long pause, he rubs his nose, says "Ummm" a few
times.

"What?"

"Now don't get all pissed off, but Dilly claims she doesn't
die."

My anger immediately reignites. "Oh, that's crap. Why
haven't we seen her around? The reason I found Ray is because we'd been bumping into each other for a hundred
years. He was the one, the only one, for three hundred more
years until we found you."

"Well, whatever, time will tell," he says. "C'mon, let's get lit
and you'll forget all about it." He takes out a bottle of eardrops.

"God in heaven, doesn't anybody around here smoke
drugs anymore?"

The mugs kick in, and I feel soft feathered wings wrap
around me. "If she doesn't die, then you should test it out,
shoot an arrow at her heart."

I hug my knees and look at Cory lying on the floor, his eyes closed. He opens them and sees me looking at him. "Oh, baby," he says and rubs his fingers on my back.

"Do you love me, Cory?"

"Uh-huh."

"Really?"

He nods.

"And it's over with you guys?"

"All done." He closes his eyes. We use some more eardrops until I feel like a doll stuffed with cotton, with no heart and no brain. I realize I'm drooling; I wipe it away. I make Cory's shoulder into a pillow and lie on it.

I said "Hi."
And she said
"Yeah, I guess I am."

The days go by like paper bags in the wind, floating down the street, crashing and taking off again. Spring has droned into summer, and I have fallen into routine. I wake up and have sex with Cory, get lit, and then kiss him good-bye when he goes off to work. If we didn't live in an abandoned building and sell toxes for a living, we could be in a serene housewife magazine.

After he left this morning, I conked out again. But in these dog days of summer, it's too hot to sleep, so I get up, wet my hair with the ice water left over in the cooler, and get lit again. Time flies by this way, probably because it takes me days to do the simplest things. It took days to dye my dress blue—I would assume I had all the supplies and get completely lit to kick off the project. Then I'd realize I was still missing something, but be too wasted to go back outside—and that would be it for the day.

I sit in the window, unable to decide if I should chew more Chill Pillz, or start to fall out of the buzz. The more I do, the hotter the letdown will be, and that can be so painful it feels like I'm on fire, and I wind up drenched in sweat. Without permission, my hand picks up the pill, pops it in my mouth, and my teeth grind it up before I make up my mind. My body is like a fiend that doesn't listen to me.

I hear scurrying sounds from downstairs. It's our "roommate" with the pet snake named Clover. Cory says he's a mute kid named Crimson, but how could he know this? I was told he's allowed to stay in the theater because he and his little punk friends figured out how to siphon plumbing into the bathroom in the lobby, and it's why we have one working toilet, sink, and a makeshift camping shower. Even though I've never seen him, I hate him. I hate his little rat friends, and I'm scared shitless of his pet snake. Sometimes when I'm lit, I think I see the snake out of the corner of my eye, slithering around the attic.

My mind gets on the hamster wheel of profound intoxicated thought, and I pedal along, thinking about how I was prepared to forgive the past, but only because I figured things would be different. There is so little change between the last time I was in Neom and this trip. We've gone from a tiny dump of an apartment to squatting in a big building. The mugs are stronger, but more expensive. Most warm days, I still go to the same park and sit around with the chains. Different color dresses, different girls, same chain system.

I sit with the blue and purple chains since we've moved up in rank. I look with disdain at the red and yellow chains who sit in a different circle, narrow my eyes at them because they mooch and sometimes they're ugly. Our chain circle is friendlier than theirs. There's more camaraderie in the cool colors because chain trades are rare once you get to this level. All the purple chains belong to Atom, and they obviously never get traded. Still, they are cautious and only refer to Atom in whispers among themselves, never calling him by name, only "him." They disclose nothing about life at the warehouse, and I can't tell if they know anything about what happened to me; they eye me with the same suspicion they would anyone else.

One of the chains in our circle told me that Ray and Dilly Dally are together. This is bad news because Cory supports Ray, and then he's supporting Dilly by proxy, and it would mean that Dilly Dally is Cory's chain, too. So I put the word out that Ray has his own deal and Dilly is forbidden from our space. Word must have gotten back to her, because Ray was gone the next day. Hopefully, when their supply dries up, she'll be picked up by a new Jack. She's pretty, she has options. But for now, I sit alone in the attic and miss Ray terribly. I used to miss him even when he sat next to me without his memory, but this is even lonelier.

These Chill Pillz suck; I'm hotter than when I started. I melt ice against my neck as I sit with my legs dangling out the big circle window, the ice sparkling like a diamond. The intoxicant industry feels stable, as the mug shortages aren't as bad because there are more types of toxes in the supply chain. But this same copacetic vibe was going on the last time, when everything suddenly collapsed during the flood. And I worry about Atom, working away like an evil hermit on the outskirts of town. Cory says he doesn't deal with him, but I know half the mugs we do are coming out of his lab.

All the roads lead to Rome. Everything breaks down to the Atom.

We chose this. I choose this. This is our solution to an endless life. If we can't physically die, we can at least be as numb as the living dead, empty and absent. These mugs slaughter time and keep us closer to death than any machete or sword.

So if I came back hoping that we would magically have some purpose to our lives, I was just forgetting that we gave up on that dream long ago.

I feel a hot flash of worry race through my body, a feeling of dread, like the moment you realize your master plan is completely flawed. My heart beats faster and my temperature rises even more, my mind swoons and I'm burning up with a fever that's spiraling out of control. Something is going to break and we'll end up in the same mess as before. What if I get torn apart? How long will it take for things to fall into chaos? When will things get so fucked up that the Workers from Over show up at our door to take me away again? The pace has quickened; we're already careening. How will I be able to forgive the past if everything is repeated?

I feel sick. I need to stop thinking. I attempt to get a handle on this mug letdown fever by putting two drops of Sart on my wrists and rubbing them together. As the clouds float into my mind, my panic gets absorbed in the soft, fluffy air and dissipates. I feel a sense of quiet, a sense that things will work out the way they are destined to. It's all good. Mindlessly, I stare at the sky. Everything is cooling down. The sky turns a dark rich blue, and I apply lip balm that makes nausea go away. Then I'm sleepy and empty of thought. It's like a magic potion, and I get the hang of it. I start to nod off.

I kill the time.

The sun gets closer with each passing day. Cory comes home in the middle of one of the hot afternoons, trashed and perky. He picks me up, spins me around, and almost drops me.

"Hey, baby, lessa party," he says, and we go to the Easy Store where a red car is waiting for us. It is boiling hot outside, but the inside of the car is like a refrigerator. I sit in the front while Cory collapses in the backseat. The girl driving has long fluffy white hair and nearly translucent skin.

"Hi!" she says, like a birdcall, and the car lurches out from the curb. She turns to me. "So you're Cory's chain, nice to meet you, I expected something different." She says this all very fast as we speed down the street. I imagine myself picking shards of glass off my face when we crash. I turn to look at Cory passed out on the floor in the backseat. I wish Cory were in the front seat and I were lying in the back. I'm sure it is much safer to be low like that.

"My name's Missing, but you can call me Missy," she says. She looks like a cockatoo with startled pale blue eyes. "We're going to me and Kota's place. We have a new toy and your boys wanted you to come." I watch the world fly by. I'm used to walking, and this is faster than the speed of light; the cars in the other lanes look like they are frozen to the ground. Way ahead, the light is yellow. She hits the gas and the car struggles, then catches on and speeds to it. I am holding on to both my seat and the door.

"So tell me about yourself, Alison."

"What do you want to know?"

"Oh, I don't know. Where are you from?"

"Over," I say.

"Where's that?"

"Far away." My voice sounds a little curt and unfriendly, but only because I want her to focus on her driving.

"Oh."

We head toward downtown, and the streets become so crowded with cars she's forced to slow down. I think I used to live around here once, but maybe not. Maybe it has changed too much to tell. Missing is mad at the traffic and changes lanes every chance she gets. There is a man in a brown dented car next to us. He seems very calm. He was next to us a few blocks ago, so I don't think this crazy driving is getting us anywhere.

"So how did you meet Cory?" she squawks in her birdcall voice. I wish Cory were awake so he could do the talking. I can't think of a lie.

"Well," I say, "after the city burned down, Ray and I were walking through the remains, and we found Cory sitting on a pile of burnt wood, so we took him with us."

She asked, and I told her.

Her mouth opens. She is wearing red lipstick like this car. "Wait," she says, "wait wait wait wait wait." She gestures like she's going to clap her hands, or indicate the symbol for something large, then she screams, "What the fuck are you talking about?"

I have just about had it with this conversation. I am stuck in a car that is so jammed in traffic that we are not moving at all. I'm done. I open the door and get out of the car and start crossing the lane of other motionless cars. Missy screams my name. The heat rises from the ground, and the air jiggles like it's underwater. It smells like smoke with a disease.

"Alison, I'm sorry, get in the car." She is leaning over, yelling out the window.

I have no idea where I am. I am far from home and have no money. I get back in.

"I'm sorry," she says. "I yell a lot. I like to yell." She looks right at me, and she looks softer. In a quieter voice she says, "I just wanted to know what city burned down. Cities don't burn down every day."

I invent a city. "Inktown," I say.

She lets it pass. "So this happened last week?"

"No, a long time ago."

"I thought you just got chained last week?"

"No. We were going out before that, but then I left." I want to say that I am not Cory's chain, but Cory's wife from long ago, before the chain system even started. "Cory never said anything about me?" I ask, feeling hurt.

"No," she says, and it is real quiet. I turn the vent of the AC so it blows on my neck. "But he could've and I just forgot," she says.

"Yeah." Change the subject. "So are you from Neom?"

"Nope. Me and my girlfriend, Kota, are from Factory; we went to high school together there. Things were fucked up, and it smelled."

From the way she says it, I have a feeling it might be best for us not to ask each other any more questions about the past. I look out the window, try to think about other things, and we slowly move forward.

Cory passes out again in the elevator while mumbling that he is alright. We untangle him and drag him to the apartment. The halls have mannequin arms sticking out of the walls, each fist holding a light bulb. It's pretty creepy.

Missy puts Cory's feet down while she looks for a key. I hear squeaking and grunting coming from inside. Missy opens the door, and in the apartment, Ray and a very tall girl with long black braids are jumping together on a trampoline the size of a hula hoop, trying to push each other off. Dilly Dally is sitting on a chair like a princess, watching all this with her legs crossed and her chin in her hand while her yellow hair streams like a waterfall over her green dress. It looks like Ray is going to win the round on the trampoline, pushing his hands against hers, leaning his body forward while his opponent bends backward, but the girl suddenly ducks out of the way, and Ray falls forward and off the trampoline.

The girl stands victorious, still bouncing a little. She has coffee-colored skin and is as tall and taut as a stretched rubber band.

"Are you Alley?" she asks, stepping off the trampoline. I nod. She comes over and shakes my hand. "Nice to meet you. You can call me Kota." She has big almond-shaped eyes and is one of the most attractive people I've ever seen.

"Cory's all knocked out," Missing says. Dilly Dally is looking at me. Ray waves at me and I wave back. We all look at Cory, plopped on the couch where we left him, his sunglasses hanging off his face. Everybody is looking at everybody. So then we all start looking at something else. The apartment is nice, with creamy carpeting. There is stuff attached to the wall, not just pictures, but objects, like a full table setting hanging from little hooks. Necklaces hang in the corners like spider webs. Stuff, stuff, and more stuff.

Dilly Dally says, "We could give him a Zip Cracker. That would wake him up."

I glare at her. She was not in my plan. Kota notices Dilly and me glaring at each other.

"Well, whatever," Kota says lightly. "I just wanted to play with our new toy. It doesn't matter if he's up or not."

"Did you get that today?" I point at the trampoline.

"Oh no," she says and raises her eyebrows, "that is not the toy, that's child's play. The new tox is much, much more fun."

Missy says, "Hey, why don't you and Dilly play a round of push hands?"

"The trampoline game?" I ask.

As Dilly and I step onto the trampoline, she narrows her eyes at me, and that's all it takes. I punch her in the face, and she is thinking right along the same lines, falling down with my hair in her hands. She slams her fist into my side, and I kick her somewhere, not sure where because my hair is in my eyes. I hear Kota say, "Good suggestion, Missing."

Ray pulls us apart, getting whacked in the process.

"Goddamn, you chains fight like cats. Now, everybody sit down and we'll settle this deal." Kota means business.

I am pouting, and I look over and see Dilly Dally pouting, too.

"Okay," Kota goes on, "Cory is trading his Cloud 9 for this new stuff called Ichorice Licorice. Missy and I have done it, and it's cool. Now, I take it Cory is gonna pay for yours, Alley?"

I nod. "And Ray's, too."

She looks at me long. "Is he also Cory's chain?"

"No, but we'll take care of it."

"Fine. Dilly, what's with you?"

"I'm with Ray."

"Is Ray paying for you?"

"No." I answer for her. "And Cory's not, either."

Ray looks confused. He and Dilly hold hands.

"I don't have any money," she says.

"Well," Missy says, "that's the way it goes, Dilly. You're free to hang out, but we can't afford to give it away." She lights up a smoke. I'm secretly thrilled that Dilly will be left behind.

We all sit quietly.

"What does it do?" Ray asks.

Kota explains, "It's a water-based tox, but it also does something to your memory, so when you come down, you won't remember anything that happened while you were on it."

"Like a blackout?" I ask.

"Right. That's even another name for it, 'Blackout Sticks.'"

"I should wake Cory up. He hates to be sober, even when he sleeps. Do you have any Zip Crackers in the house?"

"In the fridge."

Cory always chews in his sleep, especially if you stroke his cheek. I get him chewing and pop a Zip Cracker into his mouth. He wakes up after a bit.

"Fuck" is his first and only word when he wakes. He staggers to the bathroom and heaves. He comes back and sits on the couch all groggy, still wearing his sunglasses and rubbing his nose. "Missy, can I have a smoke?"

"It's a strawberry."

"That's alright." He lights up. "So what's the deal?"

"We're all going to adventure out except Dilly Dally," I say. Cory nods. Dilly looks at him, but he doesn't look back at her.

"So how do we take it?" Cory asks.

"It's pretty gnarly," Kota says.

Missy and Kota nick each other's legs with a straight razor and then twist the cap off a bottle that looks like nail polish. Each girl brushes some mustard-colored liquid over the cut on her leg. They clean off the blade and hand it to Cory, and already they are blinking slowly, holding hands.

Cory and I look at each other with the same concern. How can we cut ourselves without the wound healing up faster than we can brush on the Ichorice? Healing quickly comes with its own set of problems.

"I'll have it ready and we'll do it fast," I say to Cory under my breath.

The mug stings when it goes on. We cover our cuts so Missy and Kota won't see them instantly heal. After Dilly brushes the mug on Ray's cut, I yank down the leg of his jeans when no one is looking.

Missy gives me a sneaky smile as I start to feel something. She says, "The last thing you'll remember is me saying, 'This is the last thing you'll remember.'"

A huge velvet wave splashes over me and carries me out to sea.

Just say no
don't mind if I do

I am feeling woozy; it is hard to sit without swaying. I lie down on the carpet, which has become a white sandy beach, and let the waves of the Ichorice ocean wash over me. They roll over my head and through my body, flowing up and down like a tide.

"The first time Kota and me did it, we barfed," Missy says.

I always find these things out *after* I've ingested the mug. The spinning ceiling fan is making me seasick, so I close my eyes and focus on the waves rolling through my body, warm and thick. Cory lies down next to me, and then everybody else is lying down, our heads in a circle. There is a nice swooshing sound in my ears.

Dilly Dally sits up and starts whining to Kota, asking her for a dose of Ichorice.

"No," Kota says.

"Cory?" Dilly whines.

"No."

Maybe she will be quiet for a while.

I turn my head and look at Cory. His eyes are closed. Turning my head the other way, I look at Kota. She has her eyes closed, too; it's like we are all sunbathing. I look back and forth between Kota and Cory because it feels good to move my head like that. Both of them have very high cheekbones, but Kota's bones are rounded, like a ski slope. Cory's cheeks and chin are sharp, and if you tried to ski down his face, you would likely die. As I am looking back at Kota, a curtain of wheat-colored hair comes down between us. Dilly is peering down at her, and Kota opens her eyes. Dilly dangles her necklace above her face. "Trade ya for this," Dilly says. It is a fairly spectacular piece of jewelry, turquoise and silver and sparkly stones.

Kota sighs. "You Flower People," she says and shakes her head, snatching the necklace. "Do you know how to make your cut with the razor? Don't cut too long or deep or you'll get seasick."

"And I don't want you puking on our carpet," Missy calls out.

"I won't, I won't," Dilly says.

After a time we sit up, feeling strong and brave, ready for adventure. We're a strange-looking crew; all of us Flower People look like country bumpkins when paired with Kota and Missy, who look like they come from the future, with their tight black pants and glossy T-shirts. We get away from the stares of apartment residents and step outside, where it is dark and hot and the air is wetter than a water-soaked sponge. The pavement of the street feels soft, as if my feet are sinking into mud. This weather makes Cory's hair even curlier, forming spiral rings that bounce as he walks ahead with Kota. Their heads are bent down and their voices hushed, trying to talk business while swerving. Ray and Dilly Dally linger behind, chasing each other in some game they've just made up, running in clumsy circles and chanting, "Glub-Glub-What-What." Missy and I walk together, in the middle of this stumbling parade.

Missy asks me dozens of questions about being a chain, and how the system works. Eventually I put my foot down and ask if she's looking to enter the industry.

"Oh no, no," she says. "I'm just fascinated by you guys, you're like . . . throwbacks."

I give her a dirty look and don't say anything.

"I don't mean it like that," she says. "I'm sorry. I mean, it's just old-fashioned, with the guys running the show and the girls—" She stops.

"The girls what?" I snap.

"Nothing. Forget it."

"Well, what do you do that's so great? How do you pay for your mugs?" I ask.

"Oh, you don't know?" She raises her eyebrows and smiles suddenly. "We're thieves."

"Really?"

"I only tell you this because you're not going to remember," she says very efficiently. "We specialize in luxury goods, and we have a man who flips them into currency for us."

"Hmmm," I say. "So what happens if you get caught?"

"We do time, like everybody else," she says.

"Well, there's the difference, Missy. We're not like everybody else. We commit the crime, but the boys do the time."

"Touché," she says.

Ray and Dilly come bouncing in front of us as we walk, jumping up and down like they're on invisible pogo sticks, pointing and saying, "Moon moon moon." I follow their fingers to the sky where the buildings end at the wall of a big cemetery. The giant moon sits in the branches of a big tree, like a glowing egg trapped in a spider's web.

"Moon moon moon," Missy says, jumping up and down like a bona fide teenager. She and Kota look tall and grown up, but they're really just kids. "C'mon," she says, taking my hands. "Moon moon moon."

I play along, in spite of myself. It feels good to hop, like bouncing around in water, the street soft and rubbery. We hop in front of Kota and Cory like crazy people, and they smile but won't jump, no matter how much we bug them. I didn't think Cory would; he's not much for making an ass of himself. I guess Kota is the same way.

We've decided to walk through the cemetery, when all of a sudden Dilly sees something and races blindly into a busy street, looking like a little girl in a nightgown running through a bad dream. A car squeals to a stop right before plowing into her, and the driver honks for a long time.

I wish that car would've hit her so we could find out once and for all if she dies or not. She keeps going, making a bee-line for a statue located on an island in the middle of a busy intersection. Ray runs after her, and we all hustle and wobble in tow. She climbs up the platform to a statue of a man who is twisting around like he's about to throw a discus. He's twice Dilly's size, and she climbs up onto his knee and slides her leg through the bend in his elbow. She wraps her arm around his neck, pulling her body close as she kisses his bronze lips. Ray is climbing up the pedestal when he sees her licking and grinding the statue. He jumps down and walks away, furious, storming past us.

Cars are slowing down to look at Dilly; this is an excellent way to get arrested by the Local Drags. We all look to Cory to go up and get her, because Ray's gone and he's the only other guy. Girls have it very tough in this town, but at least we don't have to do stupid shit like climbing up and getting

Dilly down from there. Cory takes a deep breath, climbs up, and pries her off the discus thrower. Dilly snaps out of it, sees all of us, and says, "Oh," then climbs down.

"Okay, let's go," she says, smoothing down her skirt.

"What the fuck was that?" Kota yells.

"It's like a habit, like everything else, y'know?" Dilly seems embarrassed and wants to change the subject. We all badger her to explain her stunt, and finally she relents and starts telling a breathless story, about a boy standing in the dark with the rain falling shiny-wet like blood, and how he left her lonely, saying, "I've said a thousand kind things I'll never say again." Then her story jumps to his overdose on Xoanon and how he turned into a statue, and she, still standing in some kind of emotional rain, feels like she could wake him with a kiss, blah blah blah, so now she sees him in every statue and wants to make their love work again. Her story just goes on and on, and I'm starting to sway and roll my eyes. I look over at Cory and think poorly of him for dating this chick.

When her story ends, nobody says anything. Dilly chases down Ray, who's probably already forgotten she cheated on him with a statue. Maybe losing your memory is the way to go.

Cory and I start walking. I look at him and shake my head.

"She didn't used to be that way," he says.

"What? Mushy Brain Syndrome from the mugs?" I say sarcastically.

"That's all I can figure."

"Ray's problems, too?"

"I don't know, Alley. I'm not a doctor."

We all head into the cemetery. While my mind adjusts to the idea of our brains turning to oatmeal from all these toxes, I'm sent farther into orbit when I realize we're in the cemetery where Cory, Alison, and Ray are buried.

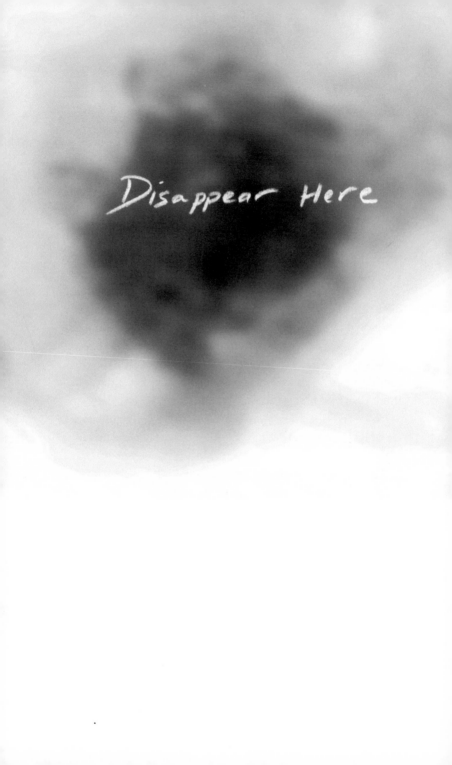

We hear the sound of bongos and follow the music until we come upon two drummers sitting next to two gargoyles. The men's dreadlocks are as long and thick as roots of a tree. They both have pale skin and muscular arms. They look a lot like each other.

They stop drumming when we get close. "Hey now," one says.

"Hey," we say. I remember these guys showing up suddenly at a nightly drum circle in the park, causing a twitter among some of the green chains, who were excited at the prospect of newcomers.

They introduce themselves as Nor and Wes, say they are from the Land of Red Clay. They are traveling the world and ask us if we have any mugs. Of course we say no, and they laugh.

"Sure, sure," says one. "I don't expect you to trust us. We are in Neom looking for a very special intoxicant. Have you heard of IDeath? There is talk of it in the Land of Red Clay." Their accents are foreign and something's not right, but Cory is all ears at the sound of a new mug. He steps forward and is suddenly friendly and helpful, listing all the synth categories, trying to figure out the genus and species of IDeath, displaying his vast knowledge of illegal mugs. Their dreadlocks look manufactured.

"There is no category," they keep repeating. "It's something completely new. It's an out-of-body experience that actually happens. Whatever you do during your dream stays in place after you come back."

"You can do anything?"

"Anything you can dream of. That is what we heard."

No one knows what to say. I don't like the sound of any of this. I bust up the silence. "Well, hey, great to meet you. Good luck finding—"

"You can go anywhere?" Cory asks.

The drummers nod. "The rumor is that all things are possible."

"That's crazy," Kota pipes up. "You're telling me I can float around, go back in time, and fuck people up like it's nothing? There's no mug like that."

"When the mugs came out that made people float, everyone thought it was magic."

I am really burning to get away from these guys. I tug on Cory a bit, and finally we leave, wishing them luck. They resume their drumming.

"That's not Red Clay drumming," Cory finally admits, once we've gotten out of earshot.

"Yeah, I know. But if they're not Local Drag officers, what are they?"

Everything in my mind spins as it all starts to click. My mug superpowers kick into action, and I remember overhearing whispers in the park from one of Atom's purple chains. She was talking about Atom stealing pharmaceutical

secrets from the government lab, and whispered of his para-
noia about the government coming after him. I try to place
the accents of the drummers with synthetic dreadlocks.

It all comes together like a puzzle: They're Undercover
Feudal Drags. They're from Capital City, and they've come
to find and capture Atom. I don't know how I put this all
together; I can't retrace my mental steps, but I'm sure of it.

I tell Cory I'll be back and don't give him time to respond.
I clumsily sprint back to the men with dreadlocks and stumble to a stop in front of them.

"I know who you are," I say, and the fake peaceful look
disappears from their faces. "I know why you're here."

They continue to stare at me and say nothing.

"The man who stole your drug formula goes by the name
'Atom.' His lab is somewhere along the outer west edge of
Runaway Village." I step close, point my finger, and hold it
in front of their faces. My voice trembles, and my hands are
shaking. "You find him. You kill him. And get that tox out of
our fucking town."

I turn around and run back to the group.


Our group is still walking; no one even realized I left. I
keep step with everyone, try to stop shaking, and let my
heart slow down. I try to get it straight. I'm wide awake
on a blackout mug and, while high, just dropped the dime
on Atom to the Undercover Feudal Authorities. Maybe not
such a smart move. But maybe they'll arrest Atom and take
him away for good, and we'll all be free. But then again—
thinking it through and knowing the tricky fucker that
Atom is—he could catch these Undercover Drags before
they catch him. And if the drags spill the beans, Atom will
know that it was me who narced him out. And to top it all

off, I'm not going to remember a bit of this. This is rich. This is brilliant. I'm so screwed, I guess I should be glad I'm not going to remember that I just made it to the top of Atom's hit list.

I try to comfort myself. What can he do to me that he didn't do already? I swallow hard, realize that he'll think of something. I decide to look at it as ignorance being bliss, and there's never much use in looking over your shoulder, anyway. I think about all these things while Cory is silent. Then, out of the blue, Cory starts explaining how we're going to remember to find IDeath after we come down from the Ichorice.

I flip out. This Ichorice adventure is turning into a cosmic clusterfuck, and I can't handle one more piece of information that will spin my brain around. I embark on a tirade about how I'm tired of watching Cory try to kill himself, then I move on to the subject of Atom, and I'm mid-lecture when Cory stops walking and holds me by the shoulders. He looks right into my eyes.

"I don't want to take IDeath to kill myself. I want to take it to go to Over."

I sit on a big gravestone, unable to stand. I feel like I'm drowning. I don't want to be on mugs anymore.

Cory tries to explain; he sounds desperate. "It's not fair, Alley. The Over Workers come, and they snatch you up, take you away from me. It's not fair that I never get to go, that I'm always stuck here. I need to know, Alley. I need to see Over for myself."

"You can't. You can't go there," I say over and over, looking at the ground and shaking my head. It's all I can say.

Long ago there were mountains in Neom—green and fuzzy mountains that looked like giant dinosaur paws. Our little cottage was there, in the crack of a dinosaur toe. Across the way were the Stone West Mountains, and Cory's name was Gideon. He left at dawn one morning and went high in the mountains with a box of poison smokes and a match. He thought if he had no sleep or food or air for long enough, the world would let him go, let him float out of his body and go elsewhere. Seasons went by, and he came back to the cottage with sunken cheeks and beaten dark eyes, but alive, always alive.

One night in our cottage, after he came back from the Stone Mountains, I was sewing and Gideon was silently staring at the fire. Suddenly he stood up and stepped into the hearth, lying on the logs like he was climbing into a bed of burning wood.

I looked up and yelled, "Oh, Gideon, no!" I went to pull him out as he was screaming and holding on to the iron grill. His skin was boiling and peeling like the bark of a birch tree, and my arms were getting torn away by the flames as I struggled to pull him out. We both yelled and howled like wolves from the pain, but we were both too stubborn to give up. "Let me go, let me go," he yelled as his eyelashes burned. There was an awful charred smell, and he started to choke. I couldn't pry away his fingers, so I dragged the grill, along with Gideon and the burning logs, out of the hearth. I stamped out the fire with a rug and sat there, panting, my palms burned to the bone. My husband was charred, much of his skin and muscle burned away. After a while my hands healed, and Gideon rolled out of the basket. "You should've let me burn," he said, starting to cough, then throwing up all sorts of black stuff and blood.

"It wouldn't have made any difference," I said. "Even if you were burned to ash, one day you'd just be back in my bed."

All the burnt muscle was coming to the surface and flaking off. His skin was growing in new and pale underneath. I swept the burnt skin off the floor while he smoked a tohode smoke. When it came time for bed, we held each other tight. He fell asleep after a long time. Then I went outside in my nightgown and cried in the cold.

"What are you thinking about?"

I am still here, still in the cemetery, still on the Ichorice trip. It all snaps back into place.

Kota is standing in front of me; everyone else is gone. I must seem glazed. She sits next to me on the gravestone. "Look at you, girl, so sad, sitting on your own tombstone," she says.

Yikes. What are the chances? This is a huge graveyard. I look at the year Alison and the boys died in the car crash. They were teenagers when they died, and now they'd be middle-aged. Too many years have passed for us to still be using their names.

"We need new identities," I tell Kota.

"Join the club," she says. "C'mon, let's get out of here."

Kota and I exchange secrets as we walk, and I can see the appeal of Ichorice. If information is as valuable as currency, then on Ichorice you can spend freely. And it feels good to talk, to let down your guard for once. When we reach the group, Ray and Dilly are chasing each other around, ducking behind tombstones. Dilly and Ray seem made for each other, with their brains turned to mush so that they can play together like children. Missy and Kota have stolen so many flowers off graves that they need Dilly and me to carry bouquets for them. We leave the cemetery and head back to their apartment, looking like a wedding procession. Once there, Missy and Cory are hard at work figuring out how they're going to remember IDeath. No one can write anything because we can't remember what hand we write with, and no one can hold a pen without dropping it. Then Cory realizes that Dilly started the Ichorice adventure after everyone else, so she'll come down later. He starts coaching her on how to tell us about IDeath. He sits across from her, like an interrogator. Dilly keeps wanting to know why somebody else can't do it.

"Because you started later and you're going to come down later," Missy says.

Dilly just isn't getting it, and Cory is growing desperate. We are running out of time; the sky is light blue and the Ichorice sea is calming. The tide is heading out.

Cory tries again. "We only need one word, IDeath. I-D-E-A-T-H. IDeath. One word. Now we're all gonna come down and we'll all be looking around, not remembering anything that happened, okay?" Dilly's eyes are rounder than ever.

He goes on. "Now, I'm going to be sitting here with a pen, and we're going to come down and be talking about how we can't remember anything." He yells over his shoulder, "Right, Kota, we'll be talking about how we don't remember anything?"

"Yeah, man." Kota rolls her eyes and puts another bouquet into a vase. "We'll all be saying, 'Wow, man, I wonder what we did.'"

"Okay, Dilly, that's when you start telling us about IDeath. Tell us it's a tox we need to find. Make me write it down. Do you get it, Dilly?"

She nods and continues to look overwhelmed.

I've never felt myself losing memories before. It's all becoming hazy; I try to remember the beginning. We cut ourselves, the spinning ceiling fan. Then what? Just as I reach to touch it, it slides away. Something about water. Something crazy and bad happened. The room is filled with flowers—roses and carnations, yellow flowers and daisies.

"Wow. Look at all the flowers. I guess we went out," Missy says.

Dilly starts yelling. She is probably still mad she didn't get to take any Ichorice Licorice. "Get a pen! Get a pen!" she yells.

"What the hell?" Kota asks.

"I'll forget! I'm going to come down!"

Missy's eyes bug, and her face gets mean. "You crafty little bitch. You stole a dose!" Dilly Dally is shaking her head, and Missy lurches for her. Dilly screams. Chaos ensues.

"Missing, stop," Kota says. "Dilly Dally, how much did you take?"

Missy lets go.

Dilly whimpers, "Something happened. Listen to me!"

Missy yells, "No! You answer me, Dilly. Where is the bottle now?"

"I didn't steal it, I traded." Water gathers in her eyes and falls as tears. "I gave you my necklace. Look in your pocket." Dilly shakes her fists in frustration. "We're gonna forget about death!" she whines.

"Forget what?" Cory is interested.

"I don't know, you said we had to find it, said it would change everything forever. You made me promise to tell you when you came down!"

"What is it?"

"Oh shit! It was, it was, death, death something, IDeath! That's it, IDeath."

"What is it?"

"I don't know!" Cory tries to get her to say more, but she

glazes over like her eyes are made from glass, and then she slumps and looks a little groggy. "I don't remember." She looks around sadly. "I don't feel good. Wow. Where did we get all the flowers?"

"I don't know," Missy says. "We were wondering, too."

"Fuck flowers!" Cory yells. "What the fuck is . . . what is it, Edeath? Edith?" Everything is still hazy and strange. I wonder when we'll get our brains back.

"Something like that; we have to find someone named Edith," Missy says.

"And it's going to change everything forever," Cory muses.

It's 10 o'clock on a
Saturday night
Do you know what
time it is?

Every time I try to fall asleep, my eyes spring open. I surrender to insomnia and replay the events of the dawn, when I got my memory back, and when we hugged Kota and Missy and said good-bye. I couldn't, and still can't, remember what happened between us when we were on Ichorice, but we all felt very close to them after the letdown. They admitted the obvious, that they're thieves, and our tongues loosened as well. I felt like I could trust them more than any other people I've met since returning to Neom.

We took the train back to Runaway Village. Cory and I leaned against the rail and closed our eyes. Dilly Dally and Ray were asleep on each other, looking cute and blond. Dilly opened her eyes and looked at me, and we looked at each other for a long time. Dilly and I must have made up during the adventure, because I don't hate her anymore. You have to give people a fucking break sometimes.

I felt like inviting them to stay with us in the theater, but didn't. They stepped off the train a few stops before us, looking like children holding hands in the gentle light as the glass doors closed and our train pulled away. Cory and I finally got home, stepped out of the morning and back into the darkness of the theater, where Ray's stars had faded away. Cory fell asleep, and now I lie here, wide awake, unable to shake this awful eeling in my bones. Something bad must have happened on Ichorice; I just don't know what.

Maybe Cory has a new chain named Edith, and this was his way of telling me. A jolt runs through me. No, it couldn't be that; he was too curious about Edith after we snapped out of it. I relax. Maybe he met a girl when we were on our adventure. After another jolt of adrenaline, I give up on sleeping. I take one of Cory's cocosmokes out of the box and sit in front of the circle window. Maybe Cory and I realized we don't love each other anymore, and it's hidden away again now. I look at Cory sleeping and light the smoke.

Poor Ray, no wonder he gets so mad sometimes. It would make me crazy to have to live without the scaffold of memory. I missed Ray so badly when I snapped out of the Ichorice; my heart felt empty for him, and I wanted to stay up, talking, asking him what to do when you hurt and you don't know why, when your eyes fill with tears and you don't know how come.

Edith is supposed to change everything, forever. But I don't know what it would mean for everything to change, and I don't understand forever. I feel like frenzied butterflies are in my stomach. Something is wrong, terribly terribly wrong. And I sense that the search for Edith is the quest for our own destruction.

I worry.


In my dream I am on the deck of a big wooden boat. A mermaid's song is floating through the air. Two Workers from Over, wearing black suits and black sunglasses, stand next to me. One takes out a gray ring box and holds it up, lifts the cover and reveals a pink pearl inside, shiny and smooth. "This means the world to you," he says and removes the pearl from the box and places it on my tongue.

I hold it in my mouth and look down to the sea that seems so far away. I spit it out, over the side of the boat, and watch the pearl disappear into the ocean foam. I look back at the men in suits, who look surprised, then I clasp my hands on the rail and jump overboard, diving into the water below.

We go late to Runaway Village. For bulk mug exchanges like this, when it's between two Jacks of the same color status, it's good form to bring your chain along. It shows that you don't want to trade anything besides the toxes. We step down the stairs to the door of their garden apartment, to a patio filled with pretty flowers in clay pots. Deodo's chain answers the door; she has big doe eyes, camel lashes, and a tiny mouth. Of course she's wearing a long blue dress, just like me. She smiles and introduces herself as May Daisy. Inside it smells a little moldy and damp, topped with the scent of incense, but it is a friendly apartment, very small, with tie-dyed curtains and music posters.

The boys close themselves off in one room to do business, and May Daisy and I start making tea. She twists off a jar lid, takes a handful of tea leaves, and puts them in a mortar-and-pestle bowl. We stand shoulder to shoulder and catch ourselves glancing at each other.

"So I heard you kicked Dilly Dally out of the roost." May Daisy's voice is soft, polite.

I am equally polite. I say lightly, "Oh, she was just a place-holder until I came back."

"That's what I hear, that you're around, then you disappear and come back, out of the blue. Where do you go?"

"It's tricky to explain," I say.

"That's alright," she says in a cool drawl. "You don't have to talk about it. And I suppose you don't like to talk about Cory trading you over to Atom last time you were here, either."

I feel my body react to this inappropriate comment, but I don't let it show. I simply say, "No, actually, I don't."

There is a silence. May Daisy starts grinding up the tea leaves, doesn't look at me. "I don't blame you. I don't know what Atom did to you, but I talked to a woman who was one of his chains way back then, and she said they could hear you screaming from the other side of the building."

"Hey, I thought you were cool with not talking about it."

"I know, I know." She looks at me, speaking softly. "It's just that everybody's curious. He did something horrible and then gave you right back to Cory. Then you split. Can't blame a chain for wondering what went down." She lightly hits the mortar bowl to dislodge the powder.

My heart is beating fast and blood races through my body, but I work to not let it show and stay silent. We hear the door opening, and May Daisy starts speaking in a light, public voice. "Hand me some of those yellow and pink petals, darlin', and we'll smoosh them in with the tea."

Deodo stumbles into the kitchen and holds on to the doorframe, rests his head on his arm. He's a very loose and relaxed person, like a noodle. The boys want us to come into the room so they can show off their stash. We finish making the tea so it won't seem like we're anxious to see it. It's bad form to drop everything and try to snag a bunch of mugs.

We carry the trays with the tea set into the room and see the floor covered with oval tins filled with something that looks like apricot jam. It's like the room is paved with little gold cobblestones. We drink tea and get lit, and the boys shoo us out again. I wish I could stay with Cory. May Daisy snatches a little oval on her way out, smiles at Deodo. As soon as we close the door, her public persona is gone. She hands me an oval tin and keeps acting like a cunt.

"Look, Alison," she says, using her hushed conspiratorial voice again, "I got traded once, too. But the chain system is changing, and you could do yourself a favor and have some currency of your own saved up. That way, if Cory blows it again and you're about to get traded, you can whip out your own currency and pay it flat out. I mean, he'll probably toss you out for stealing from him, but it's better than gettin' traded."

I hold the oval to my eye for too long. My eye stings and one eye cries as I hand the tin back to her. "Go fuck yourself. Cory's not just my Jack, and I'm not a collateral ball-and-chain whore like you; we have a thing for each other. What happened with Atom was a mistake, and it's not going to happen again."

Unfazed, she holds the oval to one eye, then the other. Two tears slide down her cheeks. "I loved my Jack, too. He looked like rain." Her eyes stay wet. "But he was a toxie and the mugs came first, and I got traded. I'm just saying it don't hurt to stash a few tins away every now and then. When you get a stockpile, I can have it converted into currency for you—"

"May Daisy, enough."

She narrows her eyes; her skin is as flawless as porcelain, and she can hide any emotion behind it. "Dilly Dally and I had a business between us. She knew better than to trust Cory. Why are you acting like you don't know better?"

"May Daisy, shut up. Shut the fuck up."

It's another day of hanging around in the park. But when the sun goes down, Cory doesn't come to collect me like he is supposed to. May Daisy and I were the only two chains left, but even Deodo finally showed up. It was after dark, but at least he finally showed. May Daisy waved good-bye, saying that Cory would probably be here in a minute, and I knew she was glad to not be the last one to get picked up, for once. The boys always check to see who is left when they come for their chains, and it looks bad to be still sitting here like a dope. Especially today of all days, as everyone's buzzing about the two Undercover Feudal Drags who were found hanging by their fake dreadlocks. Murder among Flower People is rare, and everyone is skittish because no one knows what the hell's going on. Everyone is taking precautions and fearing a Feudal raid in retaliation. Yet here I am, looking unchained in the park. The last bit of the Okey Dokey slides out of my bloodstream, and I feel cold and shaky. Summer has darted out the door, and a cold autumn chill has snuck in without saying anything. I fleetingly think about getting a new Jack, someone other than Cory. Then I remember suddenly that Cory is the reason I am stuck in this stupid system. Finally, I am forced to break protocol and walk home alone.

I know the attic will be empty, so I head straight to the catwalk to hit the mug reserve. I walk down the hall, past the box seats and the projection booth, and almost crash into someone. I'm so startled, I yelp. I am face to face with an equally startled little nymph with calico hair who looks like a girl. This must be Crimson, the kid with the snake who lives in the projection booth with his little fucking plant. He is so tiny, too fragile to be out here in Runaway Village. I've seen ones just like this getting carried out dead on stretchers.

I growl at the little thing, and he scampers away like a small animal.

I gather the edge of my dress in my hands and pile up some toxes from the hiding place backstage. My dress works like a basket as I carry it all back up the stairs. I suck down a skinny bottle of Cloud 9, and when the soft cotton feathers wrap around me, I stumble around the attic, practicing what I am going to say to Cory when he comes home. One key point is about how he passes out next to me every night and it makes me feel old, and then I lay out a couple of tough comments about him never being around. I practice the argument with the air because I am not good at fighting with Cory. I collect all the things I want to say as I knock back bottles of Cloud 9. Then I start the fight again, from the top, and then I can't remember what we were fighting about. I tell the air that I'm tired of all this.

I wish Cory were home.

I pile up the blankets and lie down, look out the window. It gets dark so early now. I will miss summer, miss the warmth. There is a safety in summer that the winter doesn't know.

Cory stumbles in. He sees my face and smiles real cute and mumbles, "Just a nap. Just a little, little nap." He makes a sign with his fingers to show how tiny this nap is supposed to be, and boom, he's out like a light. So much for our fight. I'm not as mad anymore, anyway, and I doze off with him.

After a little bit, Cory wakes me up by touching me. I guess it is a nap after all. I wrap my arms around his neck, my legs around his waist, and do what I'm supposed to do.

Light from the window stirs me awake. Lying on my stomach, I open one eye. Cory is not there, but a flock of white paper doves rests on his pillow. I smile and brush them off, hold his pillow like a lover between my knees.

I start the day by getting lit and watching a spider weave a web. I'm too scared to kill it and worry that if I let it out of my sight, it will crawl on me. So I sit hypnotized, staring at the master craftsman weaving a spiral pattern.

Ray comes home, out of nowhere. He sees the spider and smashes it with his shoe. Oh well, I guess when you're a little bug, that's just the way it goes sometimes.

I'm excited to see Ray, but he's come home with troubles. Wet-eyed and swaying, he starts tearing apart the room, looking for something. He digs through the box we use as a table, throws around the mats and the pillows. A bottle of powder gets knocked over and spills, but I don't say anything, stand aside as he storms out of the attic. I watch from the balcony as he rushes down the aisle of the theater, looking under seats, digging through the junk on the stage. I meet up with him as he bursts into the projection booth, giving Crimson the shock of his life. Crimson looks scared, even with his snake wrapped around his waist and neck. It sticks out its tongue at Ray. Crimson has a lot of little boxes and crates that Ray is dumping out. Crimson doesn't say anything, just moves from the crate he was sitting on to his table with the little plant.

I say, "Ray, what are you looking for?"

"I don't know."

"Did you lose something?"

He dumps a box of bottle caps on the floor. "I guess so." He doesn't look up.

"C'mon. It's not in here."

He looks at me suddenly. "Do you know where it is?"

"No. But I don't think it's in here."

"Fine," he barks and walks past me in the doorway. Crimson's girlish face with dark, hollowed eyes stares at me as I close the door. Poor little thing.

"Ray, you don't even know what you're looking for."

"Well, I'll know it when I find it because I'll stop looking." Boy, is he mad.

He leaves the theater, and everything is silent.

I put on my new, thrift-store winter dress and heavy rain cloak and head for the park, unescorted, to find Dilly Dally, figure out what happened.

The only chain I see is a yackety red-dress chain named Sofia. Everyone else has left because the sky is dark from the rain about to fall. I ask her if she knows where Dilly is. "I don't know, probably Atom's."

"Atom's?" All the blood rushes to my face.

"Yeah," she says in a nasty way with her nasty face. "You didn't know? Atom's adding her to his link of chains. It's happening tonight at the drum circle in the field, unless it gets rained out."

Goddamn Atom. Everything breaks down to the Atom.

I cut through Runaway Village toward the warehouse where Dilly stayed. If I don't find Ray and bring him home, he'll look for her forever. I pass a video game arcade where Cory does some of his business, and duck in. I step into the muggy dark with the deafening booms and electric shots. My eyes get used to the dark, and I find Cory standing at a station, playing a game, the colors reflecting on his face.

"Cory!"

He looks at me, not surprised and not pleased.

"What's up?" he says flatly and goes back to his game. I suddenly notice the girl who is standing by Cory and staring at me. Her hair hangs like string, and her face looks like it was carved out of stone and no one bothered to smooth out the sharp spots. Cory doesn't look up, only mumbles, "Savannah, this is Alison. Alison, this is Savannah."

Whenever a bunch of bad things happen at the same moment, my brain gets so crammed that I just feel numb, like nothing is real. The world suddenly becomes a perfect replica of itself, with characters acting out roles in some other universe. This girl is not happening, Ray is not lost, and Atom is not nearby.

I say, "Ray's looking for Dilly. He's a wreck."

"So? He'll find her."

"No, he won't. She's getting chained to Atom."

"Oh." He presses the button a bunch of times, and three things that look like bugs explode. "What do you want me to do?" He looks at me like he doesn't know me.

"I don't know. I thought you were his friend or something. I'll see you at home," I say, stepping backward in shock. Cory goes back to his game, so I leave.

Thunder and lightning break the sky, and the rain really starts to come down. I pull the hood of the cloak over my head and try to be invisible as the neighborhood gets cruddier and cruddier and I get soaked and cold. I feel like Ray as I walk the same painful steps in water-soaked shoes.

Finally, I see the warehouse with all the jagged broken windows. Outside, Ray is soaking wet, looking in the Dumpsters. He starts to lift a lid, and I push it down.

"She's not in there," I say.

A film of sadness passes over his eyes. "I'm going inside."

"No, Ray, she's not in the warehouse anymore. She's not even in this part of town."

His face twists up. "Where'd she go?"

"Aww, Ray," I say and hug him in the rain. He is shaking from the cold, and then shaking while he cries in my hair.

The pain in our hearts travels back and forth, trying to find a home. I cry with him. So many times the things that hurt the most are the things you don't remember, can't put a finger on, or feel like you don't have a right to feel. And it sucks to have to give up looking for something because you know it's gone for good.

I say, "Ray Ray Ray," and stroke his wet hair. My voice cracks. "Sweetheart, sometimes you lose something that means the world to you." The sky yawns wider, and the rain pours down. I wrap my cloak around both of us, and we go home.

I light the stubs of candles, and we change into dry clothes. We put a blanket around us and watch the rain through the window, like a movie. Ray's eyes are blue and wet, and the candlelight sparkles on them like sunlight on the ocean.

We've been out in the rain so long, he's sobered up and his memory is working. We talk about what happened with Dilly Dally, and he asks, "Who was before Dilly?"

"Nikki," I say. "There were four of us: you and Nikki, Cory and me. When we came down from the mountains, not too long after we burned the village, Nikki didn't stay with us. It's like she walked down the mountain and just kept walking. She never settled down."

"No, it was you. You were Nikki, and when we came back from the mountains, it was a city, and you became Alison."

"No, Goosey, you've got it all wrong. We've been over this. Cory is my husband; Nikki was your wife."

"It was you," he says, steadfast. "Remember? And it was long, long before then. We were in Neom when it had a different kind of name, when it was just a clump of houses. And then there was the accident that should've killed me, but instead I just stood up. It was when the laws of nature were first starting to break. People didn't understand the rules of physics, anyway, so when strange things started happening, everyone was running scared and thinking there was a weird curse on the world. You've got to remember this, Alison; it was big. Our neighbors pegged us as demons and kept trying to kill us. 'Member? Remember when I was strung up, and you were burning at the stake, and we waved to each other?"

I sort of remember giving Ray a friendly wave while burning, but it's fuzzy. My mind is going.

He continues. "So we headed up into the mountains and burned down the whole goddamn place with fire arrows. When new people came, the village turned into a big city. Years and years later, we came back down, took new names, and no one was the wiser."

"Where was Cory?"

"Cory was the child we found. He was a little kid with crazy red hair, sitting on a pile of smoldering logs and eating orange embers like they were candy. You picked him up, put him on your hip, and took him with us."

I put my head in my hands. I'm feeling panicky at my inability to remember huge events.

"That was just some little toddler."

"Popping glowing embers in his mouth? Laughing at the sizzling noise when they touched his tongue?"

Ray stands up, frustrated with me. His cowboy boots make a wooden noise as he crosses the floor. "I'm kicking back a Cloud 9; you want one?"

"Wait, Ray. Don't. I want to figure this out. I don't want to go back to zero. You're the only one I can talk to about this stuff."

"I'm not feeling so hot; I need something." He grabs a bottle and takes a swig. "The person I was had to go away, Alison. You were my girl. I would never have done this to you, this—" He gestures with the bottle, takes another swig. "Fucking chain system, using you as collateral in mug deals. I could never be . . ." His eyes are glassing over again. "What's his name . . . ?"

He holds on to the slanted ceiling for support, looks out at the rain. He finishes the bottle, looks at me, and says, "You were my girl."

And Ray is gone again.

Going nowhere fast

Cory wakes me up like the theater is on fire. I sit at attention although I am still asleep. He's hopped up on jumping beans, pacing the room, and talking a mile a minute about vampires. Not your everyday garden-variety vampires, but ones who know Edith and have some sort of mental puzzle for us.

"This will make you understand," he says and hands me a squishy bean that tastes like ash when it dissolves. He says he needs my help because he's not good at mental puzzles that let you access the corners of your mind.

Suddenly, with the help of the jumping beans, Cory is making perfect sense. These people with sharp teeth can help us find Edith. Edith is what's missing in our lives. Our lack of Edith is what's wrong with us. We must do this; it is our destiny.

We're ready for the challenge. We feel like we can take on anything. Luckily, all my clothes are the same color and match beautifully as I throw on layers of clothing. Ray is so anxious to get moving, he almost jumps out the window.

We could take the train, but hell no, we flag down a cab and race to the vampire's address. We pull up to a flimsy little brown house. No castle for these vampires, I guess. A husky woman answers our knocking. Her skin is deathly pale, and her teeth are sharp and yellow. Her vampire man is tiny and thin with the same skin. They could use some sun. They lead us into their dark house, all the windows boarded up, and offer us a seat on furniture that makes a crackling sound when you sit.

These people are clearly not vampires. They're just a couple of drips who went to a wacky dentist to screw up their teeth. The vampire-poseur lady is giving some long, drawn-out speech that I am having a hard time following. She is trying to speak, I suspect, with an accent from an earlier era—but I lived through that time and nobody talked like that. The little vampire guy pipes up, his balding head glowing in the light of a black candle. My mind wanders around their messy room, complete with a cluttered dusty shrine in the corner, loaded up with murky crystals, medieval knickknacks, and other clichés. I wonder if they worship Satan. I wish she would get to the point. She's saying something about how the answer to what we're looking for is deep inside our minds, and we need to go through a maze to unlock ourselves—and that's how we'll find Edith. Cory is bouncing his knee and biting his fingernails clear off, and Ray is nodding his head to some very fast beat only he can hear.

The little guy leans over to me. He's so creepy. "The secret of Edith," he whispers, "is in the soul of thee, thee needeth only to speak to thy soul."

"So what's your point?" I bark.

The vampires seem a little shaken. I think we were supposed to be spellbound by their little talk. I hope to hell Cory didn't give them any coins for this.

They explain there is a labyrinth we must go through.

"So is Edith at the center?" Cory asks.

"No," she whispers, "but at the center you will know."

"How? Is it written down or something?"

"Trust us," they say in unison. "You will know."

This sounds like a big pile of horseshit to me, yet we still go into their cruddy, overgrown backyard. They have set up a white paper structure, as tall as our bodies and supported by dowel rods and clear tape. "Go in and you'll see," they say from the doorway of their dark house. They need to add some vegetables to their diet.

We start the paper maze, shuttle down a white paper hallway, and turn, then turn again. It breaks off in two directions. Cory asks, "Which way should we go?"

"How should I know?" I say and look to Ray, who just shrugs. We pick a direction, then pick another. We hit a dead end and all explode in anger. Maybe on Tin Tin this could have been fun, or dreamy and playful on Cloud 9, but right now we are jumping on the beans, and we have no patience for this kind of crap.

"Let me get something straight," Cory is almost yelling. "What. Is at the end. Of this maze?" We are all stupefied.

"I don't think there's jack shit at the end of this. Even if we could find it," I answer.

"I say we haul ass," says Ray.

"Okay. Good thinking, Ray," Cory says. "Now, how are we going to get out of here?"

"Like this," Ray says and rams his head through a paper wall. We follow, tearing the layers of paper. We get out at the other end of the backyard, jump the fence, and press on.

The weather grows colder, and the big equinox celebration is tonight in the tiny forest outside Neom. Neom used to be a vast forest, with a small area cleared out for people.

But now it's all cleared out for people, and the wild trees are confined to a small wooded area with a fence around it. The boys and I bundle up our clothes, load up on mugs, and ride the train, feeling as if we're snaking through the clouds. From the train we catch a ride from a busload of Stone Folks also going to the equinox celebration. Stone Folks are like us Flower People, just wearing different uniforms. They dye their hair rainbow colors and poke lots of holes in themselves, while we Flower People sport flowing, unwashed rags. The two cultures claim to dislike the other, but there's lots of mug trading and interdating between the groups. During the equinox celebration, our differences are forgiven and the two groups party as one. We ride on their bus, sharing our Cloud 9 and drinking their Cigma Shots. We raise our glasses high in the air and cheer, sway shoulder to shoulder while singing a drinking song. The sun has set by the time we arrive at the forest gate, and we follow the sound of drums down a dark, wooded path, using lanterns made of candles and plastic milk cartons.

By a big fire raging in the middle of a clearing, Stone Folks are milling around, while Flower People are drumming like thunder, and a group of girls with the same long hair and long dresses as mine are dancing. So many girls are spinning that they disappear into the blackness of the woods. They are all trance dancing, whipping their heads in a circle so their hair's flying around like a halo, their skirts billowing out. From above, they would look like a crowd of spinning umbrellas.

A memory suddenly overlays the scene—a memory from when? When we came down from the mountains? I suddenly remember that we didn't immediately resettle in the spot that later became Neom. First we left the region with the Jahui-Yip Caravan and traveled with them, getting high on fungus and trafficking across the land. It's probably where we first got hooked and became criminals, where we learned how to leave the past behind—just pack up the caravan and ride away. The years we traveled with the Jahui-Yip Caravan were our best years; things were loose and light, just making music and dancing around the fire. It was a party like this. Why did we stop? Why did we leave?

The rhythm of the drums pulls me in, and I leave the boys so I can be with the dancers who whip their hair like tornadoes, the buzz in my brain begging to get thrown around like that. I start slow and the drum beats inside me. Everything disappears; all that's here is my body turning round and round and my hair whipping twice as fast. Then that disappears, too, and it is just the world spinning out of control.

I feel as if I've woken up after a hundred years of sleep.

Cory has been drumming while I dance. I take a break, and a few boys come up to me to start a conversation. Cory quickly appears at my side and whisks me away. I love when Cory gets a little jealous and territorial; I like him being reminded that he's not the only one who would want me. We go into the dark, between the trees. I lean against one, and it feels like a strong, lost friend. Cory leans in, sandwiching me against the tree, and we kiss long, smoky kisses that I wish the other chains could see. I'm lit up after all that kissing, glowing like fox fire as we head to a different part of the forest.

We run into Kota and Missy and do an impromptu mug trade, Sart jars for Ichorice. I don't know how they do business on Ichorice; they're both in a haze, and I can barely make out a word they're saying. I understand that criminals are always on call, but I don't know how they can even steal a glance in the state they're in. Yet The Thieves seem to manage fine, saying "Ta-ta," and staggering on to the next thing. Then we see May Daisy and Deodo. Cory always complains to me about Deodo, says he doesn't know whether to scratch his watch or wind his ass, but tonight they are both just two blue Jacks sharing unspoken comfort with each other. Deodo takes us deep into the pitch-black forest, and we feel the trail by someone calling out when they bump into a tree.

Then there is a light, and a fire inside a makeshift shelter and people inside. We join the circle of Jacks and chains. Everyone has glassy eyes and is either slumping or leaning. All sorts of mugs are being passed around in a circle, from hand to hand. When someone goes too slow, there's a mug pileup, and everyone makes fun of them. It's a blur of toxes, glass jars, and ornate pipes, along with special boxes that the Jacks saved for the equinox. Everybody is very generous when they all have their own stash, and there are so many things to breathe, smoke, nibble, or lick.

I am bamboozled. There's a line you cross when you can't feel the effects of the individual mugs; they all blur together. I could just about fall over. Some people are lying down, and I see where they're coming from. Some couples lean together like cardhouses. May Daisy and I want to talk to each other, but the boys are between us, so we end up with our feet by the fire, my head on Cory's lap and May Daisy lying next to me with her head on Deodo's lap. We can talk this way, between the boys' knees. We make fun of their lack of fashion sense—they both have the same striped, baggy pants, tie-dyed shirts with plaid flannels over them— no sense that you don't mix patterns with stripes. We have the giggles, and we laugh like little girls at a slumber party, our heads on soft pillows. More things get passed above us. Some are dangled in front of our faces, like a mobile. Above us, the boys murmur, and above them are the treetops and a sickly, burnt orange sky.

A tube is passed to me and I suck it in. I don't know what

I expected, smoke maybe, but when a liquid hits my mouth, I am surprised. It's hilarious.

"Do you even know what you're doing anymore?" May Daisy asks.

I shake my head no. "Do you?"

She shakes her head and says no, and it is the funniest thing we've ever heard. We don't know what we're doing anymore; it's tragically hysterical. We laugh and cough and laugh until we start to cry, tears streaming down our faces. We calm down, lean on our elbows, and with our faces close, she whispers to me about Dangelina, the only purple chain in the underground mug trade network. She's the only source of information about Atom's warehouse lab.

"She said Atom's been working in his lab, obsessed with a tox called IDeath. That sounds like the 'Edith' you're looking for, doesn't it?"

"It's gotta be that," I say. "It figures that it's just a stupid tox we've been running around looking for. What does it do?"

"It's some kind of lucid, out-of-body experience, where you go anywhere and can do anything. But it's not a dream; you're actually in a different reality. Dangelina says Atom doesn't even know for sure, says he got part of the formula when he went out east. But here's the thing, and you keep this quiet: everybody who's tried it has died quicker than lightning—but now he thinks he's fixed it and might be looking for new people to test it out."

I am so glad Cory can't hear this—it would be like giving an assassin a loaded gun. His body rumbles as he continues to murmur with Deodo. In the pit of my stomach, I know something happened on Ichorice, and although the memories are hidden somewhere, they're sending me cryptic smoke signals in the form of a horrible dread.

After a long pause, May Daisy asks, "So what do you think?"

"I can't think," I say and collapse back onto Cory's lap. I look at her and shake my head. "I don't know."

I don't know what to think, because I can't think. And I don't know is all I know. The punch line of the joke is a girl who doesn't know what she's doing anymore. Big hot breezes rush through my body, followed by icy chills, and the mugs keep getting passed over my head.

# three people make a conspiracy

Well.

That didn't work.

May Daisy and I are standing at the harbor, not believing a rocket just flew overhead, carrying the shipment of mugs we were planning on hijacking.

I'm tempted to try to rethink our stupid plan, where we started, and where it went wrong. But I know, at heart, it was just a pipe dream about taking control of our lives by stealing the one thing Atom really cares about.

I guess it started this morning when Dangelina spilled the beans about the shipment coming into the harbor. Atom must have really done a number on her, because she was in the park, wasted and livid, giving May Daisy instructions about how she could sabotage Atom's whole operation. She said the key ingredient for Atom's IDeath drug was coming into the harbor today, and then she and May Daisy started hatching a plan to hijack the shipment and hold it hostage. Dangelina has a dangerous amount of information—she might not know I'm immortal, but she wove me into a plan that entailed me getting run over by a truck, then shot, and then popping back up from the dead and screaming like a banshee.

In retrospect, I don't know why I agreed to it.

The harbor is walking distance, so I guess we were going to try to grab the cargo as it came off the boat—in from the Eastern Sea through the Great Lakes. But we had to get lit first, so of course we were late, and . . . then what? They didn't put it in a truck, right? The plan assumed the cargo would travel by boat then get shipped to the warehouse in a truck. I was supposed to distract them with my resurrection from the dead while May Daisy grabbed a case of IDeath's secret sauce.

Whose plan was this, again?

Anyway, none of it happened because they fucking packed it into a remote-controlled rocket and sent it shooting into the sky toward Atom's lab. Holy shit. We were so fucking outmatched. I remember Atom from when he was a young kid, rising through the ranks—but even then he was shrewd and wanted to be involved in the details. I remember how elaborate his lab was, like the lair of a self-taught mad scientist.

We stood in the middle of an empty street and watched the low-flying rocket *whoosh* overhead and disappear, brilliantly avoiding all the Local Drags on the road.

May Daisy flips open a lid and empties out things that look like candy into my outstretched palm; then she bends her neck back and shakes the last pills directly into her open mouth and starts chewing. I do the same, having no idea what I'm taking and not caring, just numbly listening to the sound of the hard drug crumbling between my teeth.

"Sweet Mother of Donuts," May Daisy says, "we lost in a way that makes you not want to fight no more."

We start walking back to the status quo at the park.

*if need be*

"Tell me," says Cory.

"No," I say.

"Tell me."

"There's nothing to tell."

"Alison, just tell me."

"Dammit, Cory, leave me alone."

He stands up and goes to the side window, resting his arm on the wall. He breathes out smoke, and it bounces off the circle window that's now boarded up again. The smoke gets caught by a draft and flies away.

"At least admit there's something you're not telling me," he says.

"I don't want to fight with you," I say.

"Fight about what?"

I sigh. "I always lose when I fight with you, okay? So let's not argue."

"So there *is* something you're not telling me."

"Stop it!"

"C'mon," he says, ashing on the floor, "I've known you for five hundred years and I can always tell when you have a secret. And you"—he points his cocosmoke at me—"are not telling me something."

Ray is looking at us like he's watching a tennis game.

"Go to hell."

"Ray, tell her to tell me."

"I have absolutely no idea what you guys are yelling about."

"Well, that's a big goddamn surprise coming from you, Ray," Cory snaps. He figures out his next move, stands in the center of the attic—the one place his head doesn't touch the ceiling—folds his arms officially, and says, "I'm going to stand in protest."

"No no no, you don't." I step in front of him and pull at his folded arms. "I'll let you stand for a hundred years. I don't care. You know what happened last time."

"What happened last time?" Ray asks.

"Well, I'll tell you, Ray." I am really ticked; my voice is shaky and the freezing cold attic isn't helping. "Cory and I were having this big fight and he stood up—just like he's doing now, like a soldier at attention—and he wasn't going to sit back down no matter what. It was the time of great heroes, and Cory was a great warrior back then, disciplined from all the time he served. We were strong people back then, Ray. We weren't stoned and soft toxies like now. So anyway, I didn't have Cory's training, but I had my iron will, and I fought back by standing right next to him, my arms crossed the same way. So we're out in the woods in our little one-room cottage, no one to disturb us, not eating, seasons changing, the two most stubborn damn people in the world. And seriously, Ray, years go by. Years."

Cory rolls his eyes and looks out the window, but Ray is enjoying the story. I cross my arms with a flourish, smile, and continue. "One day, years later, as the two of us are standing there like a couple dopes, staring straight ahead,

Cory starts to slowly turn his head toward me. It's making this horrible cracking and squeaking noise. So then I start turning my head to look at him, just as slow, with the same creaking noise going on. And I can see Cory is yellow and thin as a skeleton, with cobwebs on his arms and dust all over his mouth. And Cory opens his jaw and croaks—" I glance at Cory as he glares at me. He hates this story.

"'Honey, what were we fighting about?' I croaked back, just as slow. 'I don't remember.' Then Cory fell backward like a log and broke apart in three places; some of him just crumbled—"

Cory cuts my story short. "Just tell me what the hell is going on."

End of story I guess. So much for changing the subject.

I say, "No. You have to trust me to know what's better for all of us."

"Why do you know better?"

"Because I'm older and I'm not as bad a toxie."

"So it's something about mugs."

"No."

"Some deal."

"Shut up."

"And if it's something about a tox, then it's got to be something about Atom, because he's the only one you wouldn't want me dealing with."

I hate arguing with Cory. I take a breath. "We've talked about this. There's no dealing with Atom. You know I'll split."

"I told you I won't, Alley; now tell me what it is."

"Cory, I'll leave, my hand to God, I'll leave." He sits in front of me, and Ray does, too. They are like two dogs hoping for food.

I sigh.

"Remember with Edith, it wasn't really Edith, it was something *like* Edith? Well, Atom's got a tox called IDeath. It's no big thing, some sort of lucid dream mug or out-of-body trip, or something."

"What happens?"

"I don't know. It's just talk. You make a wish and you lie down and it might come true, or you might end up dead."

"Oh. Far out," Cory says, far away. Everything is really quiet. No one says anything.

I hate arguing with Cory.

I always lose.


One morning, there was frost on everything in the attic. So we bought garbage bags filled with ugly old clothes, and I cut them into pieces and started to sew them together into a huge messy quilt that would be ten layers thick. We'd all fit inside it like lint in a pocket. Ray found a construction site and came up with the idea of cutting a hole in the ceiling and making a chimney and fireplace for the attic. The boys went back and forth with shopping carts of bricks. I was promised an indoor stove, but remained suspect. I would've rather they worked on insulating the walls so it would be warmer right away.

Last time we went into Runaway Village, rumors about IDeath were swirling around everywhere. The mug had already gained mythical proportions, feeding everyone's hopes at the prospect of getting one wish from a genie in a bottle. The possibilities of what you could do boggled the mind. The boys and I worked on winterizing the attic, and the tension between us grew stronger as the weather got colder. Cory mentioned IDeath once, and we immediately broke into an ugly argument, screaming that we hated each other, hated our lives, hated what we'd become. I threatened to leave, he threatened to welcome it. Whether those words were instant truths, or lies said in anger, it didn't much matter; they wounded us just the same. We calmed down, and Cory quietly said that we had nothing left to lose, that we'd been whittled down to little more than dumb, hungry animals. Ray brought up quitting, and I rolled my eyes, explained that we were like crabs in a bucket. Our herding instinct is so strong that whenever one of us tries to climb out of the quagmire and get clean, another of us will pull them back, just so we all stick together.

We have quit quitting.

"Alley, we could make a wish that we know would come true," Cory says for the hundredth time, and I refuse to acknowledge him once more. Because talking about IDeath means talking about Atom, and if Cory is willing to do to me again what he did to me before, then my love for him will die. It can't be an option, not if he loves me.

We work on the attic in silence. Our only contact with one another is through passing mugs around and getting someone's attention when your arm is outstretched. I miss the mountains. I miss Nikki. She was a good wife for Ray and never lost her senses. She would know what to do now. I have become so compromised I no longer trust myself.

The silence is maddening as the days pass in the freezing attic. It's true that we have nothing to lose, and at the rate we're going, we'll all get Mushy Brain Syndrome, and none of us will be able to function. More terrifying is how I've started to fantasize about my own IDeath journey, about using a mug that will break us out of this invisible vice, and then Cory and I could have the love we once had. Without realizing it, I've become a junkie for hope.

The boys are laying bricks for the bottom of the chimney, and there's cement powder all over the place. Cutting a hole in the roof is going to be a huge mess. I look up from my sewing, watch the boys, and wonder what they would do on IDeath, what they would wish for. Then out of the silence, in that moment, Cory lifts his head and asks me to tell him if Over is the same thing as dying—yes or no. I tell him the whole point of dying is that you never come back, ever. So if I come back, Over must be different.

He doesn't ask anything else.

"Cory, is that what you'd want to do? Go to Over?"

He nods.

"Of all the damn things, Cory. Truthfully, wouldn't you just want to die? Hasn't that been your goal all these years?"

He rolls off his knees and sits back into a squat, looks at me, and says, "The second prize of a fatal overdose wouldn't be bad. But my first choice would be a reason to live."

"Why would Over possibly be a reason to live?"

"You change every time you come back. You always look the same, but you're growing up on the inside. You're passing me by, and I don't want to get left behind." He looks at the floor. "The whole time you're gone, I look for the Workers from Over who took you away. I try to find the unmarked train. . . ."

I love Cory. This is all so sad. I melt and put down my sewing and go to him, kiss him, touch his shoulders. I turn to Ray. "And you, Ray? What would you want to do?"

Ray looks back and forth between Cory and me, his sad eyes watery and blue. He looks like a lost cherub. He touches the corner of his eye and rubs his nose.

"I want my wife back," he says.

"And what about you, Alley?" Cory asks.

I stand up and go back to where I left my sewing.

Cory says, "Alison, I know you're trying to be a good hip-pie, but you need to be honest about what you really want."

Ray pipes up, "Your hate is like a moth that eats at you from inside."

I glare at the boys and then put my head in my hands and take a deep breath. Ever since I heard about IDeath, I've been secretly converting myself, telling myself that if I could go back in time, I could move forward, dreaming the dream of no longer being paralyzed by the events of the past, or living numb from the poison I'm taking, just to try to forget.

"Just admit it," Cory says.

"Fine. Fine. I admit it. I want revenge. And I want my egg back."

There is a reverberation in the air from a bell that cannot be unrung—once I set my sights on revenge, I can never go back. The truth hangs in the air, and we look at one another in silence. Then we all return to doing what we were doing, and no one says a word for a very long time.

We take a break from working on the attic to get lit and figure out what to do next. Cory says when we do the deal with Atom, he and Ray can also be offered up as collateral, as there is a market for young boys. But I know Atom will insist that I be put up as a chain as well. He will want all of us on our knees. I tell Cory I can't let this deal get decided without me, not this time.

I say, "When we talk to Atom, I'm coming with. I don't care what the rules of chain trades are; if I'm putting my soul on the line again, I'm going to be a part of it."

Cory says okay.

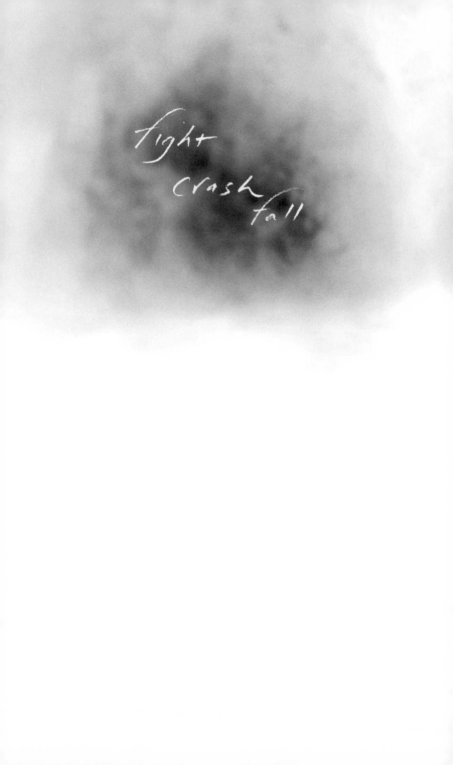

Two thugs on motorcycles pick us up in front of the Easy Store. Cory and I each get on the back of a bike and ride down the street side by side. My eyeballs sting from the freezing wind, and I don't want to hold on to my driver's waist, so I clench the bar on the back of my seat and keep my eyes closed, cursing Atom for not having his men pick us up in a car. When we get to a red light, Cory's thug flashes his blinker to turn while we stay in the middle lane. Now I know why Atom chose the motorcycles. I scream to Cory, and we reach for each other to pull ourselves off these bikes before we get split up. Cory's driver glances over and hits the gas, leaning the bike into a hard turn as they race off in another direction. Cory twists around on the bike, looking at me like he doesn't know what to do. We helplessly go our separate ways. I try halfheartedly to scramble off the motorcycle as we speed down the street.

Goddamnit. I knew it. I knew it.

My thug and I get into a very awkward scuffle as he tries to keep me on the motorcycle while we jet down a deserted street, going through red lights. I know I could jump off the bike and heal on the street, but this is what I must do. Atom only does things on his own terms. The driver calls me a bitch and tells me I'll see my boyfriend soon. He won't tell me where we're going. I stop fighting, try to figure out what to do, and regret counting on Cory for protection. I regret a lot of things. Being stuck on this bike, heading off alone to meet Atom, is only the tip of the iceberg of the variety of ways I'm screwed.

So we ride. My butt is completely numb, and I am frozen stiff when we reach a beach. The motorcycle thug parks the bike and points to a group of five men standing on the sand, wearing dress pants and overcoats. There are sea gulls circling and crying overhead in the cold air. I trudge through the sand, trying to distinguish Atom from his bodyguards. The last time I saw Atom, he was a young man, and he's aged so much I don't recognize him until I'm practically standing in front of him. He's smaller and his shoulders are starting to bend. His hair has gone from yellow to ash white, and he's bald on top. His skin is starting to wrinkle, and it's changed his whole face.

"Where's Cory?" I demand, my heart thumping so hard I feel like I might collapse.

Atom approaches me as if he's seeing a ghost. "You look exactly the same." He stares at me, then his eyes travel up and down my body as he speaks absentmindedly. "Your man is coming, but I wanted to talk to you alone for a moment, to reconcile after our last meeting."

I stand and glower.

He continues, "Should you get traded again, I assure you the terms would be very different. My alpha chain position is filled, but there's a second-ranking position that you would—"

"No. Stop. I don't even know if we want IDeath, anyway. It sounds like complete bullshit. And anything we do, we pay up front."

Atom's expression changes, and he says, "Let's check you for eavesdropping bugs."

A bodyguard with a crew cut steps forward holding an ear scope. I remember this guy's rocky face from last time. I yell, "Not him!"

Atom makes the connection and gestures for a different bodyguard to do it. The man looks into my ears and steps off when he's done. He signals to Atom that I'm clean.

Atom says, "I had figured if one of you would be wearing a bug, it would be Cory rather than you. You seem to be somewhat"—he makes air quotes with his fingers—"'out of the loop' when these deals are made."

The bodyguards produce two plastic outdoor chairs and place them in the sand. Atom gives a polite gesture for me to sit.

"Always the gentleman," I say sarcastically.

Atom's eyes flash and he freezes. "No one is forcing you to be here. No one has sold you to me this time. So sit. "

So we face each other on our two chairs in the sand, the wind blowing harder. Atom pulls the lapels of his coat closer, like an old man with chills. I'm so burning mad, I don't feel the cold.

"First of all," he explains, "IDeath is not bullshit. The early users showed signs of actual travel. The places to which they traveled indicated that a visitor had been there."

"But they never made it back."

"That's correct. But since then the formula has been improved, and the expectation is that the journey can be survived."

"So you need us to test it."

"I don't need you for anything, Alison. The youth in Runaway Village have already run away from their homes of origin. It is of little consequence if they disappear from this place, too." He shakes his head and continues, "You toxies never cease to amaze me with your disregard for your own lives, and your own bodies."

I say nothing.

"Quit glaring at me like I'm the bad guy here. Remember, Alison, Cory brought you to my door. He handed you over." He smiles. "You act like I'm the enemy, but your enemy has been beside you all this time."

I never remember moving so fast. I jump up, grab the chair, and smash him with it, knocking him out of his chair and onto the ground before his bodyguards can protect him. By the time they pull out their guns and hold them to my head, I'm on top of Atom with my hand on his throat.

Atom's voice is hoarse from my choke hold; he wheezes to the guards, "She doesn't care about the guns."

They grab me quickly and a fight ensues. Weapons are brandished and it's fairly intense. It takes all four of them to restrain me.

"Enough!" Atom screams, straightening his coat. "Eighty-three thousand quo for three marbles, three journeys. Take it or leave it."

"This is my drug. You made it with my body." I'm still struggling. If I can get loose, I'll kill Atom. One bodyguard is on either side of me, each holding an arm. Atom steps toward me. Our eyes lock at that moment, and we realize we're in the exact same formation as the last time. Atom stops. He takes a step backward.

"Let her go," he says, hauling his chair upright and sitting down. Then he puts his head in his hands, runs his fingers through his thinning hair. He looks vulnerable. His voice is quieter. "You were sold, Alison. Whatever happened during that trade, and whatever I acquired, is my property."

In spite of everything in my power, tears form and fall down my cheeks. I quickly wipe them away.

Atom says, "Our last trade was unfortunate. I needed an ingredient to keep the body alive while the customer left it. I did what I had to do."

"You stole my soul just to make a stupid tox."

"What?" He looks genuinely confused. "Steal your soul? You mean . . . that organ? Who do you think I am, the Devil? For Chrissakes, Alison, this city can bend the laws of nature, but this isn't some mythical land. What I'm offering you is more than a mug, it's a chance to fix your situation and get out of the mess you're in. You're a beautiful girl, Alison; you could have anything you wanted, if you could just get out of this place."

"You're fucking jealous," I say. "You and your fucking shrinking skeleton and your balding head, you're so fucking jealous, you need a harem of young girls to try and feel young."

"Fair enough." He throws up his hands. "Tell me how you do it, show me how you never get old and never die, and I'll give you enough IDeath to rank purple and rule Runaway Village."

"Aagh! Atom, I don't know! If I wouldn't tell you before, when you had me in your lab with your fucking scalpel out, then I probably don't fucking know, okay? All I knew was that I couldn't bear children. That was all. And my first husband got old and died, and I stayed the same. I was on my own until I found Ray, and he was immortal when I found him. It's probably just like everything else in this place; it's a mutation, just an extra couple of organs. The question you need to be asking is why do YOU die? Why is your DNA inexplicably crumbling? What's wrong with your body? That's the question, Atom. Maybe you're the freak. Maybe you're the one who deserves to be hunted."

He sighs, exasperated. "Whatever. Eighty-three K-quo if you pay up front, which you'll never be able to do. The other option is the usual system—I'll front Cory twenty additional marbles, with payment due before the first sign of spring. If he can't come up with the coins by then, you'll be surrendered to the warehouse. This is a once-in-a-lifetime offer, as you immediately get a lifetime tolerance after one trip."

He extends his hand, but I won't shake it; I've touched that thing enough already.

"I only want one dose. Then I'll have everything I need."

I have said too much.

Atom looks at me very strangely, and I turn around and walk through the sand to the motorcycle.

*So the wind*
*won't blow it all away*

Okay, here's the plan.

WE SELL 23 BLOBS OF TWEAK EVERY DAY OF WINTER

SELL EACH BLOB @ 100g RETAIL.

65g PROFIT / 35g IS OUR COST / BLOB

1500g EACH DAY PROFIT FOR 40 DAYS

OUR COST TO DEODO EACH DAY IS 805g

TOTAL EARNED EACH DAY 2300g

1,495 IS DAILY PROFIT × 40 DAYS = 65,000g FOR ATOM

2 BLOBS FOR PERSONAL USE.

Atom wants 83,000 quo for the IDeath, but we know he'll take 65,000 quo if we pay up front. We just have to exercise restraint and stay focused on our goal. With a high-margin mug like Tweak, we'll save up money, pay for IDeath outright, and no one has to be put up for collateral.

Ray and I huddle together inside the quilt as Cory does a demo of Tweak for us. He sits in front of a glass container the size of a shoe box. It's like a postmodern hookah with a tube and a pipe bowl on top. Cory scoops a blob of red jelly into the bowl and lights it while sucking on the tube. The chamber is filled with indigo smoke that separates into purple smoke that rises and blue smoke that settles on the bottom. Cory slides a little handle until it is level with the blue and purple intersection. When he hits a button, a shelf flips up, separating smoke layers, and Cory sucks out the purple smoke. The blue smoke remains in the case. In a strangled voice, he gives the following explanation while holding the smoke in his lungs. "The purple smoke is the good stuff; that's what you want. And the blue smoke is called 'blue nothing.' It will get you lit, but it'll make you sick. You put up with it when you're jonesing and willing to compromise." He finally exhales a sickly, sweet-smelling smoke.

Ray and I share one box of purple smoke, and we zip along at jet speed. We are a living paradox; we're so burning hot it's like we're about to freeze to death, and we have so much energy we sit and do nothing, just chatter on about all our big plans, congratulate ourselves for still being able to do all the necessary math for the Tweak Financial Plan. We are excited. We talk about all the things we can do on IDeath. We talk about making a new life for ourselves, about getting a nice warm house, and cutting down on the mugs. Cory starts to scoop out another blob.

"Hey, no, stop, dude," I say. "We've already done two blobs. That's all we're allowed or we'll smoke our profits."

"Oh, shit," Cory says and stops mid-motion. He sags for a second, then straightens up. "Umm, okay, you know what; we'll do one more and then I'll charge fifteen extra quo for two blobs that I sell. Same difference." He's talking fast and has a teeth-clenching look. "That's the problem with this stuff; once you start, it's a little hard to stop." He looks sheepish, fires up the bowl, sucks down the purple smoke, and the blob is gone.

Our eyes meet and he looks away.

Winter comes—BOOM—in the middle of all the Tweak. Of course, the project to build a chimney and stove in the attic is abandoned, and we begin to freeze. The quilt I kludged together is faint defense against the cold, and if we were mortals, we would have died ten times over. It takes us until midmorning to thaw. We're selling too little and smoking too much of our Tweak inventory, and it's slipping away with very little currency set aside. Cory dove into Tweak like he was falling from the sky. I'm extremely resentful; every time I feel like smoking an extra blob, I think about Atom, my plans for revenge, and it holds me back.

Cory and I unravel. We start to argue, and then all we do is fight when he's home. I scream and throw things as I accuse him of setting me up to get traded to Atom. Cory says I'm using him for the mugs. Ray just sits in the corner, his memory completely fried. He can barely speak, just gets up occasionally to stagger like a zombie toward the Tweak box, and I get up and pull him back down to the floor and hold on to him for warmth.

The winter is endless and relentless. The currency we had saved goes to buy more Tweak. I try to stash some away to sell to May Daisy, but Cory notices immediately. We fight like snarling animals. Ray is frozen in a ball on the floor.

Cory and I stand facing each other, doing a mug from a glass jar. He takes one last pull and says, "I gotta go," like he's on schedule for the first time in his life. He hands me the glass and kisses me while I stand like stone. I stand at the top of the stairs, looking at the door he walked through as the mug sinks in. Any feeling of safety or sanity that was in the room a minute ago is now gone, like it snuck out the door when Cory left. A nightmare courses through my veins, and I stand frozen. My head rotates slowly to the glass cup in my hand. The buzz that sang in my head has turned into a high-pitched electrical ringing in my ears— all those promises about Tweak are lies. The buzz starts to pulse and intensify. I feel like I'm a pane of glass about to shatter from a vibration in the air. Something inside me begins to crack, radiating like ice breaking on a frozen lake the moment before the ground gives way. I look at the glass in my hand and can't figure out how I'm able to hold on to anything while so numb and frozen. Maybe they're not even my hands; Cory could have traded me away by now, and they might belong to someone else. The glass jar falls to the floor and shatters like a bell breaking. My legs buckle, and I follow the broken jar to the floor. All around me, broken glass; pieces of light glint in the shards. My eyes fill with water, and the whole scene trembles and shimmers, like stars in a universe made of rain.

I can't sleep and I can't wake up. It's freezing. I stay in the quilt and whimper when an icy draft blows in, but still don't wake up. I can't keep my eyes open. I'm beat. When I try to get up, every part of me feels sore and I go back to sleep again. The days are mixing together like voices in a crowded room, and I can't make out what anyone is saying. Half awake, half asleep, I think we are traveling with the Jahui-Yip Caravan again, and I'm waking up freezing in the cold night, alone, because Cory is sleeping with another woman. I keep thinking we're back there, and I'm wanting to go home.

Ray is wandering around the theater in a daze. When Cory does come home, he yells and freaks out, pacing about the attic and looking out the peephole he carved in the wood of the boarded-up window. He's always enraged and paranoid now, trying to understand where the toxes went. I watch him with one eye open when he's around. He says, "Jesus, Alison, what the hell?" as I lie under the covers. I tell him to leave me alone. Sometimes he will lie next to me, and I will put my hand to his chest and feel his heart racing. He hasn't slept in weeks. He gets more fragile as the winter goes on. He is trying to make the Tweak last by smoking the blue nothing, the blue smoke that gets you high but makes you sick, and he vomits a blue mucus that reeks and freezes to the floor. "C'mon, get up, get up," he says, and I sit up for a moment and crash back down. "Talk to me, Alley; I need someone to talk to," he says.

The toxies are howling in the street from pain. The winter has shut down the mug dealing in the park, and the kids are freezing and starving to get high. Crimson is sneaking his friends into the theater, and I can hear them downstairs as they scurry around like mice. We have nothing to spare, nothing to sell. I keep thinking Clover, the snake, is slithering around the attic, taking our mugs.

Everything has gone up in smoke. We were supposed to have money for winter; we were supposed to save up for IDeath and stop the gnawing inside. Instead we have nothing. A thousand years of living and still we have nothing.

The frozen snap finally passes, and there is silence on the street. Cory comes under the covers with Ray and me, trembling. His voice shaking and cracking, he says that it's run out. The Tweak. It's all gone. We're broke.

We take turns having nightmares, all three of us under the same blankets thrashing around and yelling to the night about things we thought we'd forgotten. We try to stay together even when we sleep, to wake each other from the nightmares as best as we can. But I can't sort any of it out, and I can't wake up enough to put my head together and make a new start. My thoughts are a mess, more tangled than my hair. It's all so overwhelming, I don't know where to begin.

Ray lifts up my eyelids. He is peering into my face and blinking. "Are you sleeping?" he asks again and again. "Are you asleep?"

I stay now in a little ball, as little as I can be, with my head to my knees, stiff and sore from being curled up for so long, like a leaf drying up. I dream that I am a mermaid, thrashing around on hard carpeting in a long hallway filled with closed doors. My scales are getting snagged on the scratchy carpet, and they are chipping off, leaving behind small circles that look like thin glass. I ache as I thrash around, drowning in air, desperate for water to breathe. This air is like an itchy dry dust that chokes me as I try to inhale. I have almost drowned, when Ray steps through a door and picks me up and carries me down the hall. At the very end, a small stream of water comes from the mouth of a stone fish. Ray lifts me and props me up so my head is tilted all the way back, and the water goes up my nose and into my lungs like a grace.

*I come
in the name
of destruction*

We have a brief respite from the cold toward the end of winter. It's a false spring, but at least the worst is over. I uncurl, knowing all hope is lost. I'm sick of watching Cory go through Tweak withdrawal, and I leave him writhing on the sleeping mat, feverish and miserable. Fuck him.

I head to the park and see The Thieves' shiny red car. When I find them, Missy says, "You look sad. We're going to a party that's sure to cheer you up."

I get in the car with them and leave.

As we drive, I notice that Kota and Missy both look washed out, their eyes dark and puffy. I ask if they are sick, or very tired, but they brush off my questions. When I speculate about contracting a spring virus, Kota loses her patience and snaps, "We're not wearing makeup, Alison; sorry to shock you with our underselves."

Missy adds, "Yeah, pretty judgmental from a girl who always smells like shit."

The Thieves come up with a plan. The Thieves always have a plan, and for this one, the first step is getting a dress for the party. I say I don't have currency yet.

Missy laughs and slaps her thigh. "You're funny, Alison," she says.

But stealing a dress like the one I'm going to need is a project in itself. They draw diagrams of the store, decide on the tools to disable the alarms, and teach me their hand signals. They have a Plan A that sounds easy, but Plan B involves a lot of running, driving fast, and hoping for the best.

They make me take a shower and brush my teeth, and we hang out at their place. I used to think this room was the living room of a large, elegant apartment, but now I realize this room *is* the apartment. Yet it's warm and cozy, and it's good to get out of the attic. We drink Cloud 9 and talk into the night, The Thieves casually leaning against each other as we swap secrets we're supposed to be keeping, like what happened with Atom, or their heartbreaking story of how they had to run from their families and their homes in Factory Town. In Neom, secrets are almost as valuable and dangerous as the mugs themselves, and the less you tell people, the better. But there comes a time to pick new people to trust, because you can't live your life being frightened of everybody.

We all start to conk out for the night before the big steal in the morning. I don't feel bad about vanishing from Cory for a while. He had it coming, not to mention that every star in the sky could count for a time I waited for Cory to come home. The couch is soft, softer than anything I've slept on in a long time.

We get up early to steal the dress, all of us feeling like crap. Then every moment is nerve-racking, the reality of theft in an imperfect and unpredictable world. The big finale of stress is a Local Drag squad car following us for half the ride back to the apartment. Once we get there, Kota throws up in the bathroom and Missy has an extreme headache.

"It's not like an office job," Missy says wearily, leaning her head back on the couch.

I suddenly become aware of the benefits of letting your husband handle the criminal element of your life-style.

Now we only have half a day to get ready. I've never worn anything quite like this. The top is rubber and fits like a skintight scuba diving suit. At the waist it slopes in a V and billows out in shiny metal-looking cloth.

Missy pulls my hair into a style called The Fountain, a big ponytail right on top of my head with a long base wrapped in silver cord, sticking straight up. Then the rest of my hair arcs out and down in all directions.

The Thieves' outfits are just as outrageous. Kota has a Cleopatra headdress of gold beads and a scarlet velvet dress that's a combination of an evening gown and a monk's robe. Missy wears green makeup and a mermaid-style dress. She can barely walk.

What the hell kind of party are we going to?

In the cab, on the way to the party, I keep my head bent to the side because my hair won't fit in the car otherwise. I could kill someone with this hair, charge them like a unicorn. I hope everyone doesn't turn and stare when we walk in. But the door is opened by a smiling girl wearing a tutu without underwear and platform shoes with little fishbowls as heels. I guess we should feel right at home.

The Thieves vanish as soon as we get in the door, and right away I have to socially fend for myself. The bartender gives me a martini glass filled with a murky mint drink.

"That's Mermaid's Wineglass. It's very tasty, so be careful," she says.

This apartment is huge—high ceilings and a wall of windows. I look out into the city in the night. Tall buildings take the place of mountains, and rows of cars, stuck in late-night traffic, curve and bend with the freeway. The brake lights of one lane look like a string of rubies, and the headlights in the other lane shine like diamonds. Cory always says that my imagination makes things more valuable than they are, so if I told him the lights looked like diamonds, he would say that if they closed the road I would lose all my precious stones. But if there is no beauty around you, you have to look deeper, find it somewhere.

I watch the people at the party and feel so different. They look older than me, and even though this outfit makes me look like I fit in, I know they don't live in abandoned buildings. I know that for the women here, their clothing inventory doesn't consist of a variety of blue dresses that they wear at the same time when it's cold. I live a totally different fashion philosophy. I live a life that's not my own.

I hope my fountain hairstyle doesn't fall over. I knock back the rest of my drink and can't tell what's leaning, my hairstyle or me. A guy with slicked-back hair and leather pants approaches, tells me he was watching from across the room and couldn't help but notice my breasts.

I escape to the next room and watch the band. The music is violently loud. It's not music, really, it's a scenario of playing every note on every instrument at the same time, all the time. But after a while, sipping on my refill of Mermaid's Wineglass, it starts to sound pretty good, loud and raw.

Two guys in front of me discuss the band by yelling at the top of their lungs. In the overheard screams, I learn that the band is called Rotisserie Chicken and the Gaping Wounds. The singer—maybe his name is Rotisserie Chicken—is a beauty. He's wearing plaid pants and has heavy chains wrapped around his waist as a belt. Even when he hollers and screams and tries to look mean, he still has a beautiful face, swan-white skin and blue eyes that complement his hair. The green hair is a very natural look on him.

The yelling men in front of me continue to tell the band's story, saying that the singer's name is Angel and he fell from the sky; that he used to have real wings, and when the band performed, he would flap like a moth over the crowd. But then he went from a bad toxie to a worse one and pawned his wings, so now he just jumps around onstage. He seems to be taking it in stride, screaming into the microphone, letting out all his anger.

The crowded room is hot, and the dress, being rubber on top, gets itchy. Kota put a lot of makeup on my face, and it's starting to sting my eyes. I leave the room and wander around, trying to look like I belong.

Missy comes out of nowhere and drags me by the arm, saying it's time to meet the host. I make her fix my hair first.

With my fountain back in business, Missy twists the handle to a heavy door, and I am escorted into a room where one older man and a dozen women are sitting around a massive, shiny black table. The walls are also shiny and dark; it's like a weird lake. Missy brings me to the man and we are introduced. Volo kisses the back of my hand and insists I sit next to him. The girls in little tight dresses grudgingly make room for me. Volo asks over and over why he hasn't seen me before. "Miss Missing, why have you never shown her to me?"

Missy just rolls her eyes. I feel like we're in a cleaned-up and fancier version of the chain system, and Volo is a metropolitan version of Atom.

There is a big glass Tweak box, triple the size of Cory's, with a bowl the size of a shot glass. Next to it is a wine bottle filled with red Tweak syrup. Volo has one of the girls fill the bowl with red syrup while another girl slides the shelf between the purple smoke and the blue nothing. He gestures for me to partake. I inhale, but I'm out of practice with Tweak. It stings my lungs, and Volo puts his hand on my thigh. I cough it all out and make a noise that's close to barfing, and the girls at the table look at me like I am a child. The next girl reaches for the box, but Volo slaps away her hand. "Let her do another."

So I do it, and it stays down and I'm really flying. The girls pass the box, and everyone starts talking to the person next to them. Volo's hand on my leg starts to crawl like a bug. I gently remove it but engage him in conversation to balance it all out. I blink a lot and listen attentively; being jaiked on the Tweak makes it easy to appear enthusiastic about his insights. Volo has gone to a lot of places, so we jabber on about traveling. He has dark eyes with dark circles underneath; he is probably a little older than Atom. I start to feel unsteady, and my head is humming louder than the room; it feels like everyone is shouting at the person next to them. Their laughing sounds like screaming, and everyone has one eye on the Tweak box as it goes around the oily black table. Volo leans over to kiss me, and I tell him I have to go to the bathroom.

"You come right back, yes?" he says.

I nod.

"You go nowhere but come back here." He looks at me like he will send out assassins if I don't come right back. I am light-headed and shaky; everything feels scary and unreal. The room feels like it's going to explode in an electrical fire. I nod my head in agreement that I will go nowhere else, then make my escape from the room.

I lean against the wall in a more remote corner of the apartment, worried Volo is going to come out and find me. I tell myself I'm effectively camouflaged in the crowd and just jaiking out on the Tweak.

It doesn't feel as lonely to be by myself; everyone looks slammed, and lots of people look just as alone while standing in a group, staring into space. At the other end of the room, Angel, the singer with the green hair, is leaning against the same wall as I am. I guess the band is done. He looks at me and I look at him and we smile. He is the age I look on the outside. He slides a step closer, his back never leaving the wall. I keep my back to the wall and try to slide a step closer to him, but my dress sticks to the wall and vibrates. Little by little, one slide at a time, never letting go of the support of the wall, he approaches. I smile, my face happy to do something besides nervous twitching.

"Hey . . . ," he says, in a very wasted, Western slur. "Do you want some of this?"

He hands me his Mermaid drink, and I take a swig and give it back. I think we are the only two people at this party who aren't afraid of spreading germs. We look at each other and blink. His skin is soap-white and clear as an angel's. They say Flower People girls are suckers for Stone Punk boys; I guess it's true. And the hell with Cory.

"You look . . ." He trails off. "A little . . . dazed."

He should talk. I say, "I'm hiding from somebody."

"Wow. Thassa drag." He takes a drink and looks at me through long eyelashes. What a pair of eyes. He says, "Hey,

I have Oxo drops . . . fucking, we could hide together and do some."

We stumble into a storage room in the back of the apartment. The bassist is passed out cold on the floor, and big boxes of band equipment are strewn around. I trip over something in the dark, grab Angel's arm for support, but he falls right down with me. He weighs almost nothing.

He yanks his arm out of my grasp. "Don't fucking do that! I have hollow bones."

"Are you serious?"

My eyes start to adjust. The room is dimly lit by the glow of the city lights far below. Angel looks angry about the revelation that he can't physically overpower me. Not wanting to dwell on it, he comes at me with a deep-tongue kissing thing, which really isn't my bag, not to mention that the Tweak put the taste of metal filings in my mouth. He starts to grope at me and puts his mouth by my ear.

He goes for my breasts, but the rubber dress is like armor. I feel protected for a moment, but then it's clear he's going to rip the rubber top apart if I don't do something. Not a very nice angel.

"Hey, umm," I say, "can we check out those Oxo drops?"

He steps off and shakes his head, mumbles, "Fucking tox whore," and gets into car mechanic mode, taking out a kit of vials, medicine bandages, and a file—the kind you use to shave down metal.

"Take off your shirt."

"It's not a shirt," I say as I begin an unzipping and unpeeling process.

He takes a nip at my breasts and then takes a pinch of stomach fat and starts rubbing intensely with the metal file, trying to make the skin raw. He crouches down, rubs harder, trying to get the skin to break open and bleed.

After a few painful seconds, I pull away. "It won't work."

"What kind of immortal are you?"

"Just a freak of nature. Nothing special."

"Let's just fuck, then," he says and starts squeezing my breasts. I am fucking hating this. I push him off, and he's so light, he's forced to move back. There is nothing more dangerous than a man who is halfway down the road of getting laid. He flies into a rage and grabs my hair, puts his face close to mine and says, "Listen, you fucking whore, I'm a soldier of God; I can rip your immortality right off you."

"Really?" I say, ignoring all the sexual tension. "You can do that?"

"Yeah." He cools down and shakes his anger off, clearly a little flattered.

"Well," I say, "why don't you make me mortal; we'll do the drops and then we can fuck. I'm just . . ." I shrug my shoulders. "Coming down, and I need a lift, okay?"

With victory within his reach, he nods and approaches me again, this time gently. He touches my hair and softly angles my neck back and kisses me there. All the excitement starts to affect me, and my body is suddenly on board. He whispers in my ear, "Are you ready to get fucked by an angel? Is that what you want? Get high and get fucked?"

My body feels like it's melting, and I just sort of moan. He keeps kissing, fondling, and whispering. He breaks the news that he's going to fuck the immortality out of me and it's going to hurt. We each take a final swig of our drinks.

He suddenly seems completely sober, standing straight and unswerving. My eyes are so foggy, I could swear he has a sphere of light around his head. As he angles me back and spreads apart my knees, he asks, "Are you ready?"

Boy, am I ready. Woozy, with hot and bothered adrenaline, he starts to fuck me and it starts to hurt. Not in a big-swinging-shlong kind of way, but a weird sting, like the venom of a spider, a poison. I'm startled and yelp at the first jolt of pain. He grabs his leather jacket without breaking his stride and shoves it into my mouth. "Don't scream. Just bite down. Don't scream."

Everything that never hurt in my thousand years of living starts to hurt now. Every stab wound that healed, every burn, every sting, all at once they happen and feel the way they should have felt. The pain starts in my groin and then radiates up and down. I'm sinking my teeth into the leather jacket, muffling a scream in spite of myself. Then it's so agonizing, I start to lift away. Something inside me is changing.

And then it's done.

He gets off me and zips up his pants. "Good girl," he says and takes out the Oxo file again. I give the "hold on a moment" hand gesture while I barf clear liquid onto the floor, not too far from the bassist who has remained unconscious through this entire venture.

I clean up with a filthy cloth I find. I'm shaky and about to go into cold shock if I don't get high. Angel says, "Welcome to the mortal coil. Let's get you stoned."

He files off the skin on a section of my stomach. The skin is red with little dots of blood. And this time, it doesn't heal. He opens a package of Oxo medicine bandages and covers the wound. Then he pulls up his own shirt and replaces the bandage on his stomach with a new one. His entire waistline looks infected and scarred from previous bandage spots.

We sit on the guitar amps in silence, let the mug settle in.

The Oxo starts to wrap around me like swan feathers. It's beautiful. It's worth it. It was all worth it. For the first time in a thousand years, I can feel my blood circulating through my body.

Angel slowly stands up and walks out of the room without looking back or saying anything.

I poke my head out of the storage room door to make sure Volo isn't around, and I find The Thieves. It's time to go. My fountain is starting to hurt.

As soon as we all collapse in a cab, I unwrap the silver cord and try to smooth down the former hairstyle, but my hair sticks straight out, like a dented sombrero around my head. Kota busts out laughing when she looks at me. She says it looks like someone's got their thumb on my fountain and it's squirting out in every direction.

She doesn't know the half of it.

It is dawn. I'm aching and ready to go home. When we get to The Thieves' apartment, we hug and wearily acknowledge the great time we had. They cover my cab ride, and I ask the driver to take me to the Nowhere Land outside Runaway Village, the place I call home.

Still out of my gourd on the mix of Oxo drops and Tweak, I climb the attic stairs while holding on to the wall. Cory's outline sits up in the dim light from the streetlamps as I stagger into the attic, wearing my strange dress, my hair gone bananas, my old blue dress crumpled in a plastic bag. I stumble; Cory catches me and helps me onto the sleeping mat.

His body is burning hot. I guess he's going through withdrawal fever. He clings so tightly, he is squeezing me. "I thought you were gone. I thought the Workers from Over came back and took you away."

The room spins out of control. I say, "Shhh," and feel a little guilty. Smelling like another man, I drunkenly pat his head. I can't say anything. I can't even move.

"You're leaving," he says. "I know you're leaving me again."

The room whips around. It spins, then snaps back to where it started, spins and snaps back to where it started. There are things I want to say, but it's all beyond me now. I close my eyes, and I hear Cory's tears sizzle as they roll down his face, over his feverish skin.

I feel myself pass out as he clings to me.

*We, the liars,*
*the Cursed &*
*the lost*

"Alley, wake up; the Workers from Over are coming. We gotta go."

The Workers from Over are already here; they've put a two thousand pound slab of cement on top of me. I can't move.

Cory keeps shaking me, and I start to wake up more. There is no cement slab on me; I just have a very bad hangover and my stomach is cramping. Cory is in a panic, trying to mobilize me before the Workers come to take me away. He's going through a historic list of horrible, almost magical things they've done to handicap me, keep me from physically escaping.

"And this time it's a bloodletting; they're trying to make you weak."

Cory's voice is high and giving me a headache. I sit up and wrench my sticky eyes open. Cory is looking jiggy. Then I see why. There's blood everywhere.

Now I'm up. There's blood all over the skirt of my fancy

dress. I'm swearing, ripping everything off in a panic, trying to figure out where I'm bleeding from. I have no wounds, I can't figure it out. I stand naked in front of Cory, turn around to see if the wound is on my back.

Then new blood drips between my legs.

I get some tissues and clean up.

Cory is still beside himself, but I know what this is. I've been listening to women complain for a thousand years.

"It's a period, Cory."

He still looks confused, so I explain the basics. But then a silence settles over us. Cory asks the question that's bouncing around my aching head: "What does this mean?"

"It means I'm going to get old, and I'm going to die."

"How do you know?"

Time to start lying. "Something feels different. I can't put my finger on it, I just know."

"Why did this happen now?"

I shrug my shoulders and pretend I have no idea. Geez, I screw *one* angel in the back room of a party and that's it for my immortality. I obviously don't say this to Cory. Instead, I sit lost in thought, while Cory is freaking out, pacing the attic, trying to figure out how to fix this. His voice feels like an assault of headache daggers. I just want him to leave so I can think and sort this through.

I remind Cory that we're down to our last few oval tins. That does the trick, and despite the withdrawal fever, he is miraculously able to summon the strength to get a new batch of toxes. Yet he continues to putter, to linger. He has thoughts; he wants to talk. I encourage him to get a move on, go hustle and get some real mugs.

He is about to leave the attic but stops; his back is turned to me at the top of the stairs. He says, "Don't leave, Alison."

"Well, I need to go to the Easy Store. We need soap."

"That's not what I'm talking about." He turns around and slumps against the doorframe like a rag doll, his hair in dirty ringlets drooping over his shoulders, his thin body lost in baggy clothes. He says, "What I mean is, go to the park or whatever, but don't leave now, alright? Things are just fucked up and I've been a shithead, but we're gonna get good again, you know? Just wait for me."

I'm irritated. He looks pitiful and I want to be alone.

I don't say anything. Finally Cory lets it go and clomps down the stairs.

With the attic finally quiet, I can lie on my back, look out the window, and think about what it all means. All I get is the empty repeating echo of the fact that I'm now mortal. I let this new reality bounce around and absorb. I suspect the excitement will pass, but knowing I'm going to die makes me feel alive. There is no more "forever"; only "a while." I feel good, feel like I'm a grown woman now. How long was the blood stagnant, not coursing through my veins? How many times will this new heart beat? I have a flash of myself living a normal life with a normal guy and having a baby. I shudder at the thought, distract myself by puttering around the attic, chewing Zip Crackers, evaporating the last of the oval tins, and trying to get my brain back. I think of the angel, my mind fondly replaying what happened. I nick my finger with a knife and joyfully watch it bleed. I'm about to make another cut, when I realize this new body is precious and delicate.

It's no longer a disposable piece of trash, but a vessel in need of my protection.

Yesterday I had millions of days stretched before me and needed nothing but a daily plan to kill each one. But today I feel a sense of urgency, counting down my remaining days. And to sit here, getting high and waiting for Cory, seems like a terrific waste of my time. Life is short, and I've got to get my soul back before I die. I've heard I'm going to need it later.

I pack a bag and head out to tell Atom's purple chains that we're ready to do the IDeath deal.

Now Cory is not so gung-ho about the IDeath trip. He gets lit and wigs out about the mortality thing, about me taking IDeath without the protection of immortality.

I give him hell. "Protected? The thing that was supposed to protect us was saving up currency from selling Tweak and paying for IDeath up front. You smoked our protection, and now we're all up for trade. I know there's a catch to Atom's deal; who knows what the fuck he's got planned, but don't you ever say that you, or immortality, ever protected me from anything. I survived, but I lost my soul and now there's less of me. I feel that emptiness every day. So I am either going to change all that on IDeath, or I'm going to die trying."

At night, when the temperature drops, all three of us go into the quilt. Ray's breathing changes as he falls asleep. I'm glad Ray is between us, because I don't want to be anywhere near Cory.

Atom was right when he said we'd never be able to save up the currency to buy IDeath up front. And he was right when he said that he wasn't the enemy. The enemy has been by my side all this time.

In the silence of the dark, Cory says, "Do you love me, Alison?"

My heart has frozen into stone. I say, "No."

This is not the
time of great

"Hey! What are the chances that we have a snake right here in the theater?" Cory says, looking up from the IDeath instruction booklet.

I raise my hands in mock disbelief. Only Atom would have written a glossy instruction booklet for a drug that hasn't even hit the market yet. Cory said Atom wouldn't speak during the pickup, as Atom is convinced the Feudals are listening in.

Cory finishes the booklet and puts it in one of his pockets, jumps up and down to stay warm. "Crimson's going to be so pissed," Cory says.

I put my ear to the door of the projection booth and listen. It's silent. We don't know if Crimson's sleeping, or gone, or what. He creeps in and out like a mouse. We drew straws, and I'm the one who has to go in there and get the snake.

We slowly open the door. The tiny room is empty, just the blankets, the rose, and Clover's glass cage. I'm glad we don't have to tackle Crimson and steal his snake in front of him. Now all I have to do is make sure Clover doesn't bite me. He looks at me and sticks out his tongue. I breathe through my fear of snakes, coo and pet him, and he seems to like me, wraps himself around my arm as I lift him out of the glass cage. The snake gets cozy and wraps his body around my waist. I wonder if he can kill me this way. I leave the lid off the cage so if Crimson comes back, he'll think he escaped. We go back up to the attic and follow the instructions about lighting a candle and having it ready.

The IDeath marble looks like a regular marble, a glass ball with a winding yellow-and-green stripe. We find the tiny soft spot on the glass, and Cory pokes the syringe in, draws the plunger, and the stripe gets sucked into the needle like a genie going through a keyhole. Cory squirts a couple of drops from the syringe. We pause, look confused, and Ray reads the IDeath instruction booklet again. I take Clover from my waist, and Ray holds him by the neck while Cory injects IDeath into Clover's underbelly. Clover wriggles like a whip in Ray's hands, then goes limp, and Cory puts him on the ground.

Cory asks Ray if there are instructions for how to get a snake to bite you. He reaches for the booklet and suddenly yells out in pain.

Clover's upper body is off the floor, and he's swaying. Blood seeps through Cory's pants, right above his shoe.

"Okay, quick, make a wish and blow out your candle," I say.

Cory blows out the candle. Clover is swaying like a reed and looking at Ray and me as we slowly step away. Cory collapses onto the mat. Ray's and my eyes go from the snake, to Cory, to each other. Finally Clover slithers down the attic steps.

Cory is breathing lightly and slowly; then he stops breathing and his body gets cold.

Ray went to Crimson's room to make sure Clover got back to his cage, having discovered glass imprisonment to be better than the world outside. He said he opened the door and Crimson was sitting there on his little crate, with

Clover hanging limply around his neck. Ray said Crimson stood up and closed the door in his face.

I guess he knows.

This night is endless. I hate sitting here. Cory asked me to wait, so I will wait, smoking coconut cigarettes, watching the smoke rise up like a ghost and float away. For the moment, he certainly seems dead, and I don't find it terribly sad. For once, just once, I don't have to watch him suffer through being alive.

Ray leaves without saying where he's going.

Late in the morning Cory starts to twitch, then convulse. He comes back shaky and freezing cold. The booklet said to give him heated blankets, but we don't have anything of the sort, so I'm trying to bundle him up the best I can, when he pushes me away and wraps the blankets around himself. He glares at me.

Uh-oh.

Cory's trying to smoke, but he's shaking too hard to do it. I try to help again, but he keeps staring daggers at me, so I step off. I sit on the other side of the attic. In time, Cory pulls it together enough to get the damn thing lit.

After a couple inhales, he says, "I went to Over."

I can tell I've got a look on my face like I've eaten a canary. "Oh yeah, how was it?" I ask nonchalantly.

"What the fuck, Alison?"

"Did you try to find me?"

"Of course I tried to find you."

"Well, cripes, Cory, why'd you go and do that? You don't spend time with me when I'm here."

"Well, I got there and nothing seemed very different at first. It just seemed like a boring town. So I tried to find you." He pauses, takes a drag, and shoots me another dirty look. "So the house . . ."

Oh shit.

"With a lawn?"

"I told you to not try and find me. I told you!" I say.

"I don't understand it." Cory shakes his head. "If that's what Over is, then where the fuck are we?"

"I don't know, baby; I've been trying to figure it out for the longest time."

Cory leans his head against the wall; he looks lost.

"So do you feel satisfied, now that you know?" I ask.

He breathes deeply and keeps looking at the ceiling. "I don't want to go back to Over, if that's what you mean. I don't belong in a normal world."

He looks so sad. I cross the room to sit by him. He touches my face. "I wanted Over to change me. I wanted to go there and come back a different person."

I nod.

"What's happened to me, Alison? I used to have honor; I used to be good to you."

I think about Cory abandoning me in the desert as he ran off with one of the women from the Jahui-Yip Caravan. I raise an eyebrow at him.

"Okay," he says, "I wasn't perfect, but I wasn't like this. This isn't who I am."

"I know," I say.

"Over was my last hope."

We sit quietly, listen to the cold wind whistle in the attic like music from a broken flute.

Cory says, after a long time, "Let's forget about Over. Those fuckers will come and take you someday, but let's just not think about it until it happens. Alright?"

I nod. Cory opens up his blanket and I come in and we hold each other.

"I'm sorry I said I didn't love you," I say. "I didn't mean it."

"Yeah," he says. "I hope you love me, Alley, because you're all I got."

Now it is my turn to do the IDeath trip. Cory thinks it's a trap and Atom has something evil planned.

"I still know how to conjure up weapons in a dream state, Cory; it's a lost art, so Atom has no idea I'll be armed," I say. "I'll be fine."

Cory shakes the instruction booklet. "There are no rules in here! Are there multiple universes, or is it a time-travel paradox? It doesn't say anything! You're going in blind!"

"Stop yapping at me, man. I'm just as good a fighter as you, and we've done dumber shit than this. You are welcome to whine about your life having no purpose, but I am willing to die trying, if it means I can have meaning in my life."

Ray is back, but he refuses to help steal the snake again. Says he doesn't remember any mute boy with green-and-orange hair and won't hurt someone he doesn't know.

Ray gets out of everything that way.

So I am supposed to get the snake, and Cory is supposed to hold Crimson back. But when Cory kicks open the door of the projection booth, I am the one Crimson jumps on. He is so petite, and I just throw myself on top of him and pin him to the floor. Crimson had piled up his boxes of possessions against the door to keep us out, and now they've spilled all over the room.

"I got it," Cory says, holding the snake and the glass cage.

"Close the door behind you," I yell over my shoulder as Crimson struggles.

"What?" Cory says.

"Do it. Go."

He leaves, and I sit on Crimson's hips, with one hand on his collarbone. I open the buttons of his many shirt layers and expose two budding breasts and a narrow waist.

"So that's why you don't talk," I say, still sitting on her. "Can't say I blame you for not wanting to be a girl." I let up on her and she cracks me across the face. I smack her back and hold her down by her collarbone again. "Now, you listen good. We'll give Clover back in a little bit and won't touch him again. And you will let it go, or I'll kick you out of this theater and tell everyone you're a girl." I narrow my eyes. "And you'll end up just like me."

I get up off her and leave the projection booth.

I am so scared.

Ray and I hug tightly. I look at Cory; I'm supposed to give him my big speech now—about fighting for justice, dying on my feet rather than living on my knees—that whole thing. But the time for speeches has passed. Ray and I are both ready to go. Cory keeps Clover in the glass cage, holding his head down with a paddle while he injects him. Ray takes off his sunglasses and puts his arm in the cage. He says, "Alison, don't be sad. I'm not who you think I am."

Before I am able to ask what he's talking about, he winces from the snakebite. He makes a wish, blows out his candle, and falls to the floor.

Now it's my turn, and we inject the snake again. I put my hand in his cage and close my eyes. My heart pounds; I hear a rustling, and then a hot pain shoots through my arm and spreads to my torso like a choke hold.

Cory quickly holds the candle in front of me. "Make a wish," he says, and I'm so groggy, I can't remember it, then I wish Atom would go away and blow out the candle.

My whole body aches and everything goes black.

I open my eyes in a completely dark universe. My mind is fuzzy, and my legs feel heavy as I stand up. I can't see anything. Then, like on a stage, some lights come up and I can see my feet. I can see my bow and arrow case on the ground. But there is no ground below me. I'm standing on nothing, and it's wobbly, like standing on a raft. I grab the case and take out the bow, try to get my arrows ready, but there's only one fucking arrow in the case. There's nothing to shoot at, and I stand clumsily, looking around, feeling panicked. My adrenaline is running so hot, I'm twitching and shaking; my heart pulses in my ears. In the distance, I see something, a tiny yellow square that gets bigger and bigger as it approaches. The square is a cube surrounded by darkness, and as it gets closer, I see that it's a room. It floats and bobs in front of me, or maybe I am the one moving.

One by one, all the details gradually emerge: a desk, files, test tubes, a table with barbaric medical instruments. It's the office in Atom's lab. Then I appear against the side wall, then a young Atom appears, then his thugs.

They have secured my body to the wall, and the thugs are trying to keep my torso still while Atom is on his knees, eye level with my stomach. He is measuring with a tape measure and marking my skin with a pen.

It's time to shoot the arrow, but my fingers feel numb and I drop it, then I wobble and lose my balance while I try to pick it up. I feel like I'm in an ocean storm. I'm panicking. There's no time. I look over and see Atom checking his diagrams. He has a long knife in his hand. He looks nervous, and he snaps at the thugs to keep me still.

I stretch open my bow as Atom moves forward with his knife. In front of me I am screaming for him to not do this. The image in front of me is mixing with my own memories, and it's fucking me up. I'm shaking and unsteady, freaking out because I only have one arrow and feel like I won't be able to shoot straight. I focus on finding my strength and pull it together. I used to be a soldier in the army, long ago, way before Cory. I have my training and my weapon. I can hit anything. I can kill Atom and stop this from happening.

I hear myself let out a bloodcurdling scream as Atom makes his first cut on my stomach. It heals up before it even starts to bleed. He grabs my hip with one hand and jabs the knife into my stomach and pulls it down, slicing me open, then reaches his hand into my torso. It's all happening so fast, and I remember the feeling of organs being moved as he fumbled for the egg. I finally get the arrow positioned on the rest when I hear an explosion—like the world crashing to the ground. It's so loud it drowns out the sound of my screaming. Out of the corner of my eye I see a burst of flame. I take my eyes off Atom and the scene in front of me and look at the explosion. A body has emerged from it and is running in my direction.

I freeze and don't release the arrow. As the figure gets closer, I see it's Atom. Atom from the present day, with his balding head and his long hair on fire, running with a machete in his hand, faster and more powerful than he could ever be in real life. I look back at the violence of the past unfolding in front of me. I only have one arrow. I can kill Atom from the now or the Atom from back then, but not both.

My mind tries to calculate which Atom to kill, but I don't have a single moment to figure it out. I don't know what to do—until I think of Atom cutting me open with a knife, right now, for the second time.

I twist my body and release the arrow. It lands in the old eye of Atom running toward me. He lunges a few more steps and collapses. The fiery explosion dies down. I turn to look at the past, and it's so gruesome I go numb—my bow falls to the floor. Atom has reached inside my body and I am screaming. I remember the pain. I remember his hand searching my intestines. And then the thing I'd forgotten: just as he gets his grasp on the egg, the wound on my stomach seals shut, with Atom's hand trapped inside.

We all freeze with shock at the horror of what we see; my stomach has healed over, and Atom's forearm is fused with the flesh. I stop screaming, and there is a split second of absolute silence. It's not clear if his hand is gone. Atom screams in terror, and I scream for him to pull it out. He uses the other hand to hold down my flesh, then braces his legs as he gets ready to yank his arm out of my body, still holding the egg inside me in his fist. In the past I close my eyes and prepare myself for the pain.

I can't watch this. I can't go through this again. I look away and wish for this nightmare to end, because it's over. I have lost again.

Everything fades to black.

And I wake up.

Cory is waiting for me when I return from IDeath. It is very dark. Once I work through the shakes, I lean against Cory and weep without pause. We pass the night like this, waiting for Ray to wake up.

He never does.

This world
will only break
your heart

Ray's body is still on the floor, and I am still waiting for him to come back. When someone is immortal, or at least seemed to be, you can't just declare them dead like other people. I remain steadfast in my belief that he just needs more time, and I weep without ceasing, burning new candles after the old ones melt away, continuing my candlelight vigil. I arrange Ray's arms so he's holding his cowboy hat to his chest. I sit next to his body, crying an endless parade of tears. Night slides into day into night, and into day and night again.

As we wait for Ray to wake up, we hear yelling and commotion on the street below. It's something about Atom, Jacks casually yelling his name without fear. Something big happened while I was on IDeath.

Cory says, "Maybe you really killed him, Alison."

"Then I'll really never get the egg back." I sniffle. I cry harder and wipe away tears with a soaked handkerchief. "And I still miss those mountains."

"I know you do." He takes a drag; his voice is as gentle and gossamer as the smoke he exhales. "But you know, Alley, you make it even harder on yourself. I know you like to look out the window and think of the water tank as a moon, but"—he flicks an ash—"when you see an object as something it's not, it can start to get heavy. It gets heavy with all the things it's trying to be, right?" I blink at him through the tears. "See, Alley? So say they do construction and take down the water tank, then what do you lose?"

"The moon."

"Yeah, the moon, when all you had to lose was a fucking water tank. The mountains were just mountains." He leans his head back against the wall and breathes. After a long time he says, "Hey, Alley?"

"Yeah?"

"Don't get mad at me, but you never even knew you had an egg inside you until Atom took it away."

"The egg was different."

"Different from what? Alley, this idea you have, that the egg Atom took was actually your soul . . . you made that up. There's no reason to believe that he did anything more than harvest an organ from you."

"Something is missing from me. I feel numb and hardened. I'm not all there anymore."

"Baby, neither am I," he says and kisses me. "C'mon, just lie down on the mats and get some sleep. I'll keep vigil for Ray while you rest."

The sun rises and falls once more. As the shouting on the street grows, we decipher the words, and come to the realization that Atom seems truly gone. We agree to have Cory go out into the world to find out what's happening while I sit shiva. He leaves, and I put two new candles on either side of Ray's still body. I get lit and lean against the wall. Then slowly, the shadows on either side of Ray start to get up. I search for heavy things to put on top of them to weigh them down, but now we have nothing of any substance. Using the blanket as a net, I try to trap them, but they seep through the holes in the cloth and reach toward Ray, steadfast. I swipe and punch; my hands pass through their translucent forms. I break a glass bottle; try to rip and scrape their slimy bodies, which feel like a mix of goo and fog, but it makes only light scratches on their blank surfaces. As they pick up Ray's limp body, each shadow puts one of Ray's arms around its shoulders, and Ray looks like he's being lifted from the ground by a nearly invisible force. His cowboy hat falls to the floor. I jump on Ray's back to keep his body down, but the shadows are strong; they trudge on, undeterred. The circle window is still boarded up for the winter, and they pull the board off with one silent tug.

The two shadows stand on the windowsill, Ray sagging between them, his arms out like a limp scarecrow and his blond head bowed forward. I grab Ray's hat. I yell to them that they can't take Ray without his hat. But it's no longer a cowboy hat; it's just a floppy leather hat in my hands.

I run back to them and leap out the window right after they jump. They float into the sky while I crash to the sidewalk below. I lie on the ground, shattered to pieces, and watch Ray float away. Having no will to pull myself together, I lie broken in the cold.

Eventually I go to the box seats, curl into a ball, and cry. I think of Ray, I think of Atom. The sadness has fallen upon me like a great clump of sludge. Through the water in my eyes, I see Ray's last, fading star. He showed me how to make winter stars by scraping the sparkle off frost and mixing it with the glare of the snow. I remember him trying to teach me how to make them, how we squatted next to each other on the sidewalk, laughing while holding a cup of snow and a switchblade. I told him he was my Ray of light, and he smiled something that shone even brighter than the stars.

Tears fall like the ticks of a clock that never unwinds. There is so much to cry about after all these years.

Cory runs into the theater with a wheelbarrow of toxes. He slams the door shut behind him and barricades it with a plank. He starts looking for a hammer and boards to nail the door shut. He's tripping. "It's fucking hot out there, fucking Local Drags patrolling every fucking block."

"Cory—"

He ignores me. "No one knows what the fuck happened, Alley. Some swat team from Capital City came in, turned the doorknob to his lab, and the whole room exploded. Pow! So Atom could be dead, he could be in jail, or he could've gotten away. Nobody fucking knows. It's chaos."

"Cory!"

"What?"

I say, "Ray's gone. The shadows dragged him off the floor and took him away."

Cory stops, looks at me, and says, "Who the fuck is Ray?"

It takes a really long time for everything to settle down. We find a new hiding place for Cory's looted stash of mugs, and we board the doors for the next few days. Atom's purple chains whimper and wander the streets, looking for toxes and a new home.

I spend hours trying to get Cory to remember Ray. At first I'm sure he's got Ray's Mushy Brain Syndrome, but Cory can remember everything else. I show him the floppy leather hippie hat that used to be Ray's cowboy hat. Cory says it's his and always has been. He puts it on his head, asks me if it looks familiar. I have to admit he's right; I've seen him wear it many times.

I pick up Ray's rainbow-colored sunglasses and say, "These! These! These were Ray's. We would walk down the street together—"

Cory says, "And you would be wearing your rose-colored sunglasses and we would trade to see how the world looked through each other's eyes."

I flop to the floor, defeated.

"Neom has gone crazy, Alison. The laws of nature are bending more and more. Just today someone was saying the Poetic Justice system is becoming fascist." He breathes. "Look, there are a thousand explanations for what you saw, or why I don't remember some dude you say I've been friends with for five hundred years—but we'll never know which explanation is right. It's just one of those things."

I sit, stunned by it all, trying to decipher Ray's last words. "I'm not who you think I am." I think about the time I brought him in from the rain, how he said he was the one who came down from the mountains with me, how I was his girl. I put my head in my hands, exhausted by sadness and confusion.

"There was no Ray," Cory says, and then, totally unexpectedly, he starts to cry. I am so surprised by this, that for the first time in ages, I stop crying myself. I sit across from him and look into his face, which he covers with the sleeves of his jacket. Cory says, "I know I've turned into something awful, Alison; I know I have. And I'm so . . . so . . . fucking sorry." He uses his sleeve to wipe away tears.

I look at him silently, unmoved. Somehow this apology has made things worse; it's so inadequate, so small and meaningless when compared to the events of the past. Cory wipes the tears with his sleeve.

"When you got traded to Atom, I felt the good part of me leaving. It's like you said about the egg, that you were lighter, and there was less of you. And if the Poetic Justice system demands that nothing be created or destroyed—"

"Maybe the noble part of you grew a life of its own."

"But now that's gone, too," he says.

We mill around the theater for hours, stoned into a solid wall of numb confusion. And then someone starts banging on one of the fire exits.

We unbarricade the door and May Daisy blows in.

"Where's Deodo?" Cory asks.

"He's at home," growls May Daisy. "Alison, I need to talk to you. And you"—she marches up to Cory—"are fired. All the Jacks are fired. The chains are officially in revolt, and we're taking over the mug trade until this crisis passes. We're taking the inventory and distributing it outside Runaway Village. We"—she points to herself—"are going to clean up the mess you made."

Cory mutters in defense when May Daisy starts poking Cory's chest with her finger. "Like how y'all had it handled during the flood? Like how all the chains got sold down the river that was flowing through Runaway Village? You Jacks did a hell of a job."

She is all charged up and pokes him with every accusation. "You boys, you Jacks, you blue-level dealers, it was your collective incompetence for which we chains paid a terrible price. And no one, no one, suffered under your hand more than your own chain." The two of them turn to look at me. I stand there like a dope.

She looks back to Cory and points at the air above. "Now you, go up into that attic and wait there while Alison and I settle some business."

Cory obeys, stunned and without words. He looks at me as he shuffles out. I stick out my tongue at him.

"It only took one chain to destroy the whole thing," May Daisy tells me. "A little, very underage daughter of a rich pappy. Her name was Coca Lola, and the Local Drags caught her naked and lit, dancing in the street. Now, you know the Local Drags were never going to arrest Atom, but Coca Lola's dad went private, got his own posse of Justice Men to push the crooked drags out of the way and just bust in. At least that's the thinking, that's the best guess floating around amongst a whole bunch of guessin.'" May Daisy pats the chair next to her and waits for me to sit down. "Dangelina said she and the other purple chains heard the raid and started fleeing and hiding and losing their heads. Dilly Dally and some other girls knew about a trapdoor and got out, but not after snagging a whole bunch of mugs from the lab. Then when the 5-0 left for a donut break, the Jacks started looting, just like Cory and Deodo did. I tell you, Alison, it's all a hot mess."

I can hear my heart beating in my ears. "So no one knows if Atom's alive?"

"No one knows. He could have been blown to bits; he could have escaped. But if he's alive, heads are gonna roll; he'll make everyone pay for looting his warehouse and showing such conspicuous disrespect."

May Daisy pulls up her skirt. There is a petticoat underneath with a gigantic stash of mugs carefully sewn on every inch of cloth. I thought I heard her clinking when she came in.

May Daisy asks if I know any girls outside the chain system who can move mugs out of Runaway Village. I smile and say I do. I feel like big-girl-boss-lady all of a sudden.

I spend the night sewing Cory's loot into my underskirt, like May Daisy did. The capsules she gave me are so extraordinary, I push it one step farther by pulling apart the casing and snorting the powder up my nose. *Hope I don't die!* The thought cracks me up, and I sit giggling all alone like a madwoman. There's no more hurt, no more fear, just energy. I feel metaphysical. I don't have a mug problem, I have a mug solution! When I think of Ray or Atom, I uncork, pop open, flip, twist, unzip, tear with my teeth, unscrew, remove the safety, pull the trigger . . . and the emotions crumble to dust. Very handy—unless, of course, I'm vomiting or feeling bugs crawling on me—but there's no sense thinking about that until it happens.

Our mug arsenal has so many tins and bags, I will have to carry the surplus in a satchel. The sun rises, and after being inside the theater for weeks, I tell Cory I'll be back in a bit. I open the fire escape door and feel the first breeze of spring.

So much has changed in such a short time. Ray is gone, Atom could be anywhere, I've been emancipated from the chain system, I'm out of love with Cory, and I'm mortal. Despite all this loss and change, I feel a new freedom, like I'm taking my first step into a new season of my life. I do one last snort, hoist the satchel of toxes over my shoulder, and head out to find The Thieves—begin my first day in a new world.

*the revolution*
*hems + haws*

Missy and Kota set up an afternoon mug trade with girls they know from out of town, a trio with exotic mugs to swap and foreign currency to spend. The Thieves call these girls The Bandits.

"But I thought you guys were The Bandits," I say.

"We're The Thieves. The Bandits are different," Kota explains without explaining at all.

The Bandits arrive and slink in like willowy triplets. They are hard to distinguish, but the ringleader seems to be the one named Ahn. The other two hang back, talking in a foreign tongue, swatting and groping each other by way of a joke. I've never seen a group of girls like this, with such smoky eyes, tight black clothes, nails like claws.

Missy wanted to do the deal, but settled on getting a cut from making the introduction. After watching Cory for so long, I know how it's done. I know our providence's market value and trade rates for each variety, and so does Ahn—so we negotiate and barter Ersilia for Teodort, Zenobael for Daspirin, and Perinz for Ottavix. Then we all gather around the table to "inspect the merchandise," and The Bandits get even wackier as we all get blitzed. I like these girls; they are hypnotizing to watch and clearly out of their goddamn minds.

One of Ahn's sidekicks asks who did my eye surgery. I have no idea what they're talking about.

Ahn's face, layered with dark eye pencil, peers into mine. "No, those are her natural shape," she says to her girls. Then she asks me, "Are you an Eastern or a Southeastern?"

"She's ethnically ambiguous," Kota answers for me.

"Ooh!" Ahn's eyes get bright, and she says in her thick accent, "That is most very popular at the Geisai House now. You must come with us to Capital City; we're to join Army of Revolution!" She smiles a showgirl smile and strikes a pose with a twist of her wrist.

Her sidekicks immediately drop their side conversation and look at me with an expression I've seen on kittens, a curious but vacant look. "We would get you into shape." Ahn reaches over and grabs the extra meat on my hip. "And teach you how to dance for men."

"Well, gosh, what an honor," I say.

"Do not act superior of me," she says sharply. "When your mugs are all traded, you will have nothing and no one to take care of you, and your choices will be few." She hands me a map. "Show this to no one. Here you find us for one month. Then we go cross the water and we are all gone."

We finish the exchange, and The Bandits blow out the door like a breeze.

When I get close to the park, I can see Cory's red hair halfway down the block. He sees me coming and jogs down the path to meet me before I reach the park.

"Hey," he says cautiously, with a careful look on his face.

"What?" Something is wrong.

"Well . . ." he continues in a soothing tone, like someone who is about to confront a rabid cougar.

"What's going on?"

He sighs and spills the beans. "Deodo and May Daisy made up. The chain revolt is over." He perks up, tries to smile. "But I can move it for you. Did you trade the mugs for the exoticants?" He reaches for my satchel and I push his hand away.

"They . . . What? They made up? What do you mean 'they made up'?"

"Well, one chain sold mugs to an Undercover Drag and got arrested; that dampened everyone's spirits." I must look crushed. "Alley, it's for the best that you girls stay out of this."

I start to walk past him, ready to raise holy hell in the park, and he stops me and holds me by the shoulders. He looks at me, calm, with a pleasant expression on his face, and says, "Alison, this place is crawling with Undercover Drags." He smiles as if he's talking about something upbeat and keeps his hands on my shoulders. "What I need you to do is put down that satchel, give me a kiss, and then skip away to see your friends." He kisses my cheek. "Unless you'd like to go to jail," he says sweetly and smiles again.

I do as I'm told and go into the park. It's immediately apparent that Cory is telling the truth; the chains sit in a circle, doing their fucking weaving, while the Jacks are on the perimeter, passing mugs to each other through handshakes.

May Daisy sits in a circle of blue-chain girls. I sit next to her and her doe eyes slowly meet mine. The big brown eyes that held all the fire of our potential are now just the storage space of a failed revolution.

"Alison," she says, soft and stoned, looking back down and groping for her weaving twine. She fumbles it with the co-cosmoke she's also trying to pick up. "I take it you heard it's back to business as usual." The blue chains in the circle are listening in. I convince her to stand up and walk to a spot where we can talk in private.

I ask, "What happened? Did he poison you with incense? It will wear off tomorrow—we can get back on track."

"No . . ." she slurs. "Deodo really loves me, you know? And I couldn't do that handshake they do when they pass the drugs. I kept dropping shit. And he feels really bad about always picking me up late—"

My throat is getting tight and my eyes well up. "So you just gave up? What fucking line did he hand you; did he say he'd kill himself if you left him? What were those magic words that made you shitcan an entire revolt?"

"He said he'd die for me."

"Oh, of course!" I almost scream. "That's new! Did he make that line up? Because every morning at breakfast, when Cory feeds that line to me, I certainly roll over."

Her eyes narrow, and she sways like she's been pushed back by the wind. "At least I didn't get fucking butchered," she slurs. "If I were you, I'd be fucking angry, too." She leans forward, waving her hand with the lit smoke between her fingers, and says, "No no no, you know what? I wouldn't have been angry, I would have been . . . *gone*. So if you're such a fucking activist, you go lead the fucking revolution."

I really want to get lit; I'm starting to jones. I feel more like crying than fighting and can't think of any cruel responses. I just tell her that if the yellow chain behind her wasn't an Undercover Drag, I'd kick her ass.

"Oh yeah? And if her narc-ass boyfriend, who can't even play Hacky Sack—if he wasn't watching us, I'd have you on the ground and be standing on your hair."

She starts to walk away, but then turns around and comes back. "And what were we going to win with our revolt, anyway? Ooh! More mugs! Oh boy!" Her voice cracks, and shaking her head, she staggers back to the group. She stumbles, then says over her shoulder, "Wasn't like a noble cause or nothing."

I cross back the way I came. As I near the blue-chain area, someone calls my name and soggily points to a group of red-chain girls sitting in a circle in another area of the park. "Somebody's been looking for you. Her name is Peppercorn."

Peppercorn jumps up as I approach and runs toward me. Itchy, twitchy, and jittery, she hustles me to an isolated part of the park, and we sit under a tree. Her red dress is in tatters, her hair stringy. She is a young one, maybe fourteen. She is rattling on, stuttering, saying she can pay me for the mugs she needs, she's got something to trade. And I'm thinking, *Oh boy, more beads.*

I feel terribly sorry for her, and sad in general; I give her a tin from the stash I still have in my underskirt so she can at least finish a sentence. Soon she stops itching, and her eyes gloss over like everyone else's. She combs back her dirty and tangled hair, telling me she can pay me. I tell her not to worry about it and give her a different oval tin. She starts to chill out.

Leaning against the tree, she says, "I have something for you, Alison; it's good."

I roll my eyes. "Whatcha got, Peppercorn?"

"This." She fumbles in her bag and takes out a notebook. "I used to be one of Atom's chains, right? I used to be purple, high all the time. Then during the raid, we were all snatching and grabbing what we could carry, and this looked like mug recipes, you know? But then I looked at it and it's all about you."

She hands it to me and sits quietly. I flip through the notebook and see an outline of my figure with a blank face and the egg drawn in with arrows and numbers. It has science diagrams and chemical compounds, things that look like notes and theories, lab notes. I do a tin just to slow my heart down.

While I look over the notebook, Peppercorn starts to rattle on again, this time something about looking for a new Jack and how dry things are. Her voice is a scratchy and soft din as I try to read. I finish flipping through the notebook and look up at her. She's still talking, to herself more than me. "But I really think things will get better and I'll be able to love somebody, just not today. . . ." She looks up, and she whispers, "Sometimes love is only sleeping."

I give her enough toxes to last her a few days, but I know they'll be gone by sundown. Stinky Peppercorn gives me a hug and goes back to her circle.

I go home to read the notebook since there's nothing to do in the park. I'm back to depending on Cory for my supply. I sit cross-legged in front of the circle window and open the notebook.

Atom's scrawled notations are completely random, starting with his justification for stealing the egg. It's glaringly clear that Atom is a complete hack. He had journeyed to the east and then Capital City and was just copying what he'd seen the mug lords and scientists do over there. And even the formulas he was copying were just wild guesses, a mixing of hallucinogens with poisons and other mugs, trying to find something they could market as a mug that would make dreams come true.

In the margins, he writes, "*Due to the relativity of time and the relativity of truth in Neom, it is difficult to determine if these three adolescents are truly immortal, or only seem ageless by the standards of a transient area such as Runaway Village. By cycling through names and filling archetypical roles, it's unclear if they are changing names, or are new inhabitants altogether, replacing themselves with new youth who are so similar they are mistaken for the original."*

As the journal progresses, it disintegrates into the ramblings of a paranoid psychopath. The fact that he would keep such an incriminating journal, which is interspersed with teenage-girl diary entries about his chains not appreciating him, makes me wonder if he has early onset Mushy Brain Syndrome.

He writes about how I narced him out to two Undercover Feudal Drags. He claims these drags, masquerading as drummers, tried to infiltrate the system. Before Atom killed them, they gave me up as the informant. Atom is insane. I never even met the Undercover Drags; I mean, maybe I was in an Ichorice Licorice blackout or something, but I doubt I would have been so stupid as to drop a dime on him. But it's what Atom believes, and the whole IDeath trip was probably his way to kill me. The guy is out for blood. If he comes back to Neom, I'll never live through it.

I close the notebook and look at the city from the circle window in the attic. The clouds sit where the mountains used to be. I used to think they looked like the mountains' ghost, haunting the horizon, but now they just seem like clumps of water vapor. The factory pipes in the distance don't pump out magic genies, they pump out filth. And the water tank is nothing like the moon. I look out into this miserable, decrepit city and feel an ache in the place where my soul used to be, and know it's just a matter of time before Over comes to collect.

I scramble for something to do, someplace to go, somewhere to run. I feel like I'm about to jump out of my skin, and I wish I could talk to someone, get some perspective.

As Mountain People we could get high and see the world from a distance. It would always help to see the land all at once, like one large, pulsing organism.

I find some Flower People from out of town and sell them a couple of weak mugs at an absurdly inflated price and use my spending currency to take two trains to the observation deck of the highest building in the city. Neom stretches out in three directions like an endless, rugged tapestry. One side ends at the beach and a smooth plain of blue water. I've always been afraid to cross the sea, afraid of the monsters in the middle—but how much worse could they be than the monsters on this land?

I forget, sometimes, how really big Neom is; seeing it stretched out like this, like a doll's city, I feel our tininess. The attic, which seems so high, is barely a bump in the sidewalk. Long ago, when we burned down the city, it was just a little thing and it seemed like a breath that would finally exhale, but it just took in a deeper breath and rebirthed itself. And no arrow could burn it down. Later the water would wash it all away, but that was later, much later. There was even a fire so strong it jumped across the river, but still the city was undeterred. Neom had grown strong, so strong it knocked down the mountains so it could grow wider and taller still.

I start putting coins into the telescopes, gazing as deeply as I can before they switch off when the time runs out. I'm studying the landscape like a map, trying to find my way. I scan our old neighborhood and look for the temple where The Oracle lives. He would talk to me, he could help. During Drug War II, he always let the soldiers in, gave them a bowl of rice and helped them practice Battle. The Oracle Kimball would always say he wasn't teaching us how to fight, but how to stop fighting. Cory was his student, but

I was his favorite, and I had come to him, even before the flood, wanting guidance.

It's dusk, the time of day when Kimball leads the street soldiers in staff practice on the temple roof. I go through a pouch of small coins, looking for them. I'm pretty sure I'm looking in the right spot, but there is a billboard on top of a new square building, not a strange little storefront temple in the middle of the city. When I had come seeking The Oracle's help, I remember thinking the quaintness of the temple architecture was so out of place, it looked fake, like a themed restaurant.

I had knocked on the door and convinced the monk to tell Oracle Kimball I was there. "He knows me, just say my name," I kept repeating. When I finally got in and told him my story, he just said, "What's the question?" And I explained more, but he'd said that unless I had a question, he couldn't tell me an answer. Then I'd ask him a question, but he'd say it wasn't the right question.

The other thing I remember about the conversation is that he thought Atom was a title, not a name, and he kept saying that Cory was trying to become Atom. He just couldn't get it right. It's like The Oracle wasn't The Oracle anymore.

The observation deck closes, and after the first part of the train ride, I get off in the old neighborhood and give finding The Oracle one more shot. But the neighborhood has changed, and I quickly get lost and sit on a park bench. I discretely do an oval, bending forward like I have a headache, shielding my face with my hair. I take a few steps to throw away the empty tin, and a bum walks by the park bench, pushing a cart of metal cans, using it like a walker. He is a tiny, thin man in a tattered purple silk suit, with a spine so curved his long beard hangs down almost to his waist. He stops and points to my little coin purse on the bench. "Is that your purse?"

"Yes."

"You can't just leave your purse like that."

"Yeah, I know."

"I had a bag of coins once, and I left them for . . . not two moments, and someone took them. Just like that."

"Hmmm."

"This is a bad town. This is the kind of place where if you let down your guard for one minute, someone will come and stab you in the back."

"Yep," I say.

"This place isn't safe. I think about catching a train and getting away." He pushes his cart and keeps going. "You're not safe here, either," he says.

I sit and keep trying to figure out what Oracle Kimball would say. Finally I give up and go home.

I go back to the attic and look out the window, wondering what I should do. I feel like a kitten stuck in a tree, looking down and waiting for someone to rescue me. Then I get lit and can't remember what I was trying to figure out. Was I thinking about leaving Neom? Was I thinking about leaving Cory? I give up; I don't know.

I sit and listen to the white noise buzzing in my mind like static, my eyes glazed over. I feel like I'm turning into stone. It is dark outside, no moon. A red car pulls up. It is a shining red, glowing in the streetlight like neon lipstick. I am mesmerized by the red color; it sinks deep into my eyes. And then it hits me—The Thieves are here.

The Thieves always have a plan, but it's not always a good one. They're working with a new crew to move their shoplifted merchandise, and they want to bring me on board because, as Missy delicately puts it, "You can't get killed."

"Hey, wait," I protest and explain The Big Change.

"Hmmm." Missy makes a wincing noise out of the side of her mouth. "Then I guess we take our chances and hope for the best," she says to Kota.

Kota looks at me. "Everyone says The B&E Boys are assholes."

"B&E?"

"Breaking and Entering. Anyway, they're having a little party. Missing, throw me the keys."

"Do I need to take a shower again?" I ask Kota.

"No, I suspect these guys smell just as bad as you. Let's get going. It's a hike, almost all the way to Factory Town."

The keys are thrown and caught, and we speed in the shiny red car toward the darkening sky.


Ixnax is a seriously ugly man. Greasy, splotched, and bloated, he could be on a public service poster that demonstrates how mug addiction makes you look like you have an awful disease.

Kota was right about the filth; the place smells like a dead animal. A handful of dirty, lanky boys are drinking around a folding table, and a few girls are sitting on a red couch laminated with grease. Beyond a couple of crumpled sleeping mats, the apartment is bare and grimy, smudged handprints mark smoke-stained white walls, and light bulbs hanging from wires cast hard and ugly shadows.

One of the guys looks up from the game. He has green hair. It's the angel I fucked at that party. Ixnax makes a few nonspecific introductions. "This is my crew," he says as he gestures to his guys. Regarding the girls wearing green tunics over black pants, with greasy, green-streaked hair, he adds, "And their chains." No one looks up, except Angel, who comes over and shakes my shoulder like we're good buddies. "Hey now," he says.

"Hey," I say back and find myself in blinking-and-flirting mode. It dawns on me that I could chain up with this guy and bail out on Cory. He's green, he's a lower rank, but what has our higher rank ever gotten me, anyway?

Everyone starts choosing their liquid mug choice from the fridge while Angel and I engage in idle chitchat. He points out Bah Bah, the Bloody Plastic Lamb. The B&E Boys had taken it from someone's lawn and decorated it as a sacrificial lamb, adding red paint for blood and accessorizing it with a cheap, plastic pearl necklace. As he proudly explains all this, I hear a toilet flush, and a pregnant girl with flat green-and-yellow hair steps out.

"This is my chain, Zil," he says as she approaches. Then I realize she's gaining speed, barreling toward me despite her belly. Her eyes are burning red, and she punches me in the face when she gets within reach.

This party is already starting to suck.


"Time to go," Kota says as Angel pulls his girlfriend away from me. Missy hisses at her that it's too early, and the two of them silently negotiate with each other by staring, glaring, and raising eyebrows. With Kota's final, silent throwing up of hands, it's clear Missy has won the negotiation, and we all sit down on the bug-infested furniture.

In the corner, Angel and Zil argue, and I keep hearing the words "second chain." Missy strikes up a conversation with Raccoon, a guy with the darkest circles under his eyes I've ever seen. Ixnax is trying to make conversation with Kota, but I can see from her body language that she's cringing from his breath.

Time stops as we hang out, building trust.

I go to the bathroom a lot and during my trips there find myself stalling, looking at my face in the mirror. My skin looks bad. I look like I belong on a public service poster, too. Suddenly, during one of my trips, a ruckus breaks out in the main room.

When I return, Kota and Ixnax look wound up, like cats with their backs arched. Ixnax is on a diatribe about honor among thieves—and what he does to people who steal from him. Kota is denying any wrongdoing, saying she never stole any pearls. As they argue, it dawns on me that the source of the argument is the worthless dime-store pearl necklace that was hanging on the plastic lamb. Everyone is watching out of the corner of their eye while acting like nothing is going on. No one steps in to help Kota.

The arguing continues. Neither will back down, and then Ixnax starts doing some bizarre breathing, with puffing, buggy-eyed weird movements, like a yogi trying to swallow a whole rope. Kota prepares her stance, ready for Ixnax to lunge.

But Ixnax doesn't lunge; he does something that no one on the planet expects: he projectile-vomits a stream of green puke right into Kota's face. The acid hits Kota's eyes, and she screams and covers her face and gives one instinctive mule side kick that lands on Ixnax's stomach and knocks him to the floor. Everyone stands there, stunned, while Kota is blinded and howling. Finally the reality sinks into Missy and she shuttles Kota to the bathroom and we can all hear the sound of water running.

Ixnax lies on the floor, catching his breath, and no one says anything. The B&E Boys and their chains all look at one another like puppies in a burning building.

I repeat: this party is starting to suck.

Ixnax wheezes for Raccoon's attention across the room. He gives a series of hand signals that seem to indicate ripping and cutting. Raccoon nods, looks at all the guys, and they file out.

Eventually, the bathroom door opens, and Kota, keeping her eyes closed, is led out by Missy, and the three of us head for the door. Ixnax blocks the door and growls, "Give me the necklace." Blinded and defeated, Kota reaches into the front pocket of her jeans and throws the plastic, beaded necklace to the floor. We are then allowed out.

On the street level, we realize the car is gone. I reenact the hand signal I saw Ixnax give Raccoon. Missy starts swearing.

"What?" Kota asks. "What does that signal mean?"

"It's the signal for the crew to take away everything we have. They took our car, and they're heading to our place to break in and clear us out." Everyone's spirits are broken as we head to a gas station so Kota can rinse out her eyes some more. They will heal, but it's going to take awhile.

I ask, "So are we still going to do a job for Ixnax and The B&E Boys?"

"Get the fuck out of here, Alison. Get the fuck out. We'll talk to you later."

On that loving note, we part. I make my way to the major trains and head back to Neom, back to Cory and my old life once more.

I let myself into the auditorium, but can't bring myself to go back to the attic. I can't be the madwoman padding around up there anymore. I'm jonesing like crazy and start digging around in some of the usual stash spots under the seats in row G. I am in a frantic search mode when Cory comes down.

Of course, gossip being what it is, he immediately starts giving me shit.

"The Angel?" he yells, his voice cracking. "You're going to chain up with someone ranked green?"

I roll my eyes and keep digging around. "Cory, where are the fucking mugs?"

"The Angel is a total lightweight. He's always got some chick sitting on his lap so he won't blow away in the wind. You can't be associated with—"

"Cory! Where are the fucking mugs?" I'm in full-blown wretched tox-whore mode, and I don't care if it shows.

"What, you fuck some green-rank douche bag and I'm supposed to hand over my stash? What the fuck?"

I stop. "Is this about me fucking another man or about damaging your status? Holy shit."

"When have you ever given a shit about sex, Alison? You only fuck when you have a motive."

"True. But I've put out for you plenty, and now I want some fucking mugs!"

I spot his satchel and make a mad dash for it. I dump it out and grab some Seo, Octomess, and Cumbia. I hold the mugs in my arms, huddled around them protectively, like an animal, glaring at Cory.

"You're disgusting," Cory says and heads upstairs.

I've been in a little fort I made, on stage left of the theater, for hours. Or days. My little habitat is made of planks, bedding, and scraps of the velvet curtain. I don't want Cory watching me from the balcony seats, judging me.

Someone is banging on the door and I'm hiding in my little fort, high and not dealing with it. Cory isn't home, so the banging goes on and on, intensifying. Suddenly there's an explosive smash and the sound of the door flinging open and whacking against the wall. I poke my head out of my fort and see Kota in the emergency exit doorway with a large, long gun in her hands.

"You shot the lock off the door!"

"Sorry," she says. "You weren't answering."

I shake my head. Cory's going to have a fit.

"Can I come in?" she says.

I stare at her, mystified. But she's looking about as shaky and three-sheets-to-the-wind as I am. Her eyes are beet red and tears are streaming down her face.

"Sure," I say. "Come sit. We have an auditorium."

"Okay, hold on. Can I bring my guns in here?"

"Ummm. Sure. Fine. How are your eyes?"

I help Kota bring in the trunk of guns she's wheeled to the theater. We sit down; she lights a strawberry smoke and leans back, draping her spider legs over the seat in front of us.

"Still sting. Our place got cleared out, and Missing and I broke up. That stings, too. My guns were in storage, so that trunk is the only thing I have now." She starts coughing, and when she's done, her voice is more hoarse than usual. "And I can't go back to stealing—that door is closed."

She looks at the stars on the ceiling. Her eyelashes have a natural curl and surround her almond-shaped eyes, glossed over with tears that roll down her face with each blink.

"You have electricity?" Kota asks.

"No, we, ummm, make the stars with sunlight that we pour into the light bulb socket."

Kota stares at me and blinks a few times. "You guys are some weird-ass hippies." She looks back at the stars and we sit in silence.

"Missing has decided"—Kota's voice chokes—"to become Raccoon's chain. Imagine that, he and The B&E Boys break into our apartment, steal everything, and then he offers to take care of her since she has nothing."

"Welcome to the chain system," I say.

"Absurd."

There is a long pause, then she says, "So, I came to let you know that I'm getting the fuck out of here. I'm selling the guns and heading north tomorrow." She inhales and breathes out smoke. "I'm going to check into a rehab and start over."

She lets the words settle. Of all the possible options—of all the scheming and planning that was on the table—this sounds very bad.

"So is getting lit out of the question?" I ask.

"No. It is not out of the question. I'm not in rehab yet."

I get out the tins, bottles, and bags, and Kota takes straws and tinfoil packs out of her purse. She flips the flame on her lighter and asks me if I ever think about quitting.

"Quitting Cory or quitting mugs?" The question just pops out of my mouth.

Kota raises one eyebrow at me, like a question.

"Mugs, no. Cory, yes," I say. "And I gotta get out of this town, too."

"Are you going to run off with The Bandits?"

I feel my eyes get wide as the mug and her suggestion kick in at the same moment. "That's a great idea! Then I won't have to be alone!"

"The Bandits are seriously wild, Alison. I mean, they talk a good game about the Army of Revolution, but those girls work in Geisai Clubs and dance for men. That's no better than what you got now."

I think about the box under the stop sign in the attic, where I saved the map The Bandits gave me. I say, "I know the Chain Revolution only lasted for one day. But that day, with my own satchel, dealing with The Bandits, making my own decisions . . . I didn't want to stop. I didn't want to go back to being hooked on Cory. I'm okay with having a mug habit, I just want it to be mine."

"But Geisai Clubs? Come on. You're just gonna bring your handcuffs with you, waiting for the next guy to clip them on."

"Yeah yeah, I know, but what do you want me to say, Kota? Men are what I'm good at." I twist open a tin lid. "So hooray for you, dusting yourself off and feeling strong, talking about quitting as you sit there with a straw in your hand. But me . . . not so much."

I bring the tin to my eye, Kota sucks off her straw, and then we swap.

"I hear ya, I do," Kota says after a pause. "And I'm sore over Missing, make no mistake, but I've tried half quitting before. So without her bringing me down, I have only two things left to quit," she says, holding up her first two fingers. "Toxes. And this city."

"What about those two things?" I ask, pointing to her other hand, with two fingers in the air to support her smoke.

"Don't be a smartass. Listen to me. This is the city they used as a test case for the new pharmaceuticals, right? And coincidentally, it's the exact same fucking place where the physics laws broke." She glances at the stars. "Maybe some sunlight is coming through the roof and lighting the stars that way." She takes out a vial with a salt shaker top, casually shakes blue crystals onto the back of her hand, licks them off, and hands the vial to me. She continues.

"Last week you were asking me about some dude named Ray and talking about new people being created out of thin air when people go bad—but shit, I don't remember meeting *you*, let alone some puffy-haired dude named Ray. I was nicking and doing little licorice drops all the time, so how would I know? Maybe he was a normal guy who overdosed and no one wants to talk about it."

I say nothing. The little crystals sizzle and pop on my tongue. I swallow them down with Cloud 9 and wonder if my stomach will explode. We look at the stars like we're watching a movie.

"I apologize," she says softly. "We can talk about something else, but I was just trying to illustrate that it's hard to make an escape plan when you're all confused." We sit in the dark silence. I don't say anything, because my throat is tight and I don't want to start crying.

"You'll leave him when you're ready," she says.

If I knew the way,
I would take
you home.

Fuck.

I'm leaking air.

There's a pinpoint hole between my shoulder blades, and I can feel a little stream of air pouring out when I put my finger in front of it. I reach around and cover it with my thumb, but then I hear a hiss coming from a new spot on my shoulder. The skin around the leak has become squishy and doesn't bounce back. A few hundred years ago, the Over Workers got sick of chasing me around, so now they disable me first.

Well, I guess this is it. Can't say I didn't see it coming.

Since I'm too much of a wimp to leave Cory, I moved back up to the attic and let Kota sleep in my habitat on the stage. I move from my spot by the circle window and press my back against the wall to try to stop the leak. I didn't want to go this way. I was just starting to feel ready to break out on my own and explore strange new worlds, but now I'll end up getting dragged off by the Over people to that colorless place.

I'm finding myself wishing Cory were here.

The last time Over came, it was all terribly quiet. Ray had carried me home after they put me in the Dumpster outside

Atom's warehouse, and he had waded across the flooded streets of the Village, my hair and dress dragging along the water's surface. When the floodwaters receded, Cory got it in his mind that we were going to live and let live, start fresh, and go to the top of Cricket Hill to watch the sun rise. I remember standing on the hill, shell-shocked, hurt, and cold. As the sky grew light, Cory talked about making a new start, about changing. I just stood silently and waited for the sun. The sky got white and light, but the warm glow of the sun never came; it was just a hazy, nothing day. And in that moment all the rest of me caved in on the emptiness, and I was left hollow.

I remember Cory talking about hope for the future, and it was so absurd I flew into a fury, took my wedding band off my ankle, and threw it at him.

"I'm leaving," I said and walked down the hill. There was a strange patch of dense mist, like a cloud at the bottom. Three ladies wearing flower sundresses and huge sun hats stepped out from the fog as I approached from above. I could see their pretty lipsticked mouths and the brims of their hats as they stood at the bottom of the hill. I had started to walk past them, not realizing they were from Over, when one raised her head. She saw me, but she had no eyes.

There was no fight left in me. They took me by the hand, and that was all.

Cory comes into the attic, stands above me, asks if I'm alright.

I pull his knees so they bend and he's sitting in front of me. I say, "Cory, I'm leaking. I have a hole in my back, and I'm losing air and getting soft."

His face falls.

"They're coming for me," I say.

"No," he says, shaking his head, starting to quietly panic, saying it's not time. When he touches my face, it dents. He pops a piece of gum in his mouth and chews frantically, then plugs the hole with it, and a beautiful silence fills the room. Then it starts again, louder, on my neck. He chews another piece of gum and puts it on. I spring two new holes, one in my foot and one in my hip.

My face is dented and I have gum on my throat. "I must look terrible," I say.

Cory's face contorts in sadness. "No, Alison, you look beautiful." He tries to say something else, but I cover his mouth with my mouth. He breathes hot desert air, and it inflates some of my parts that were crumpling, but it also makes the hissing stronger. I sit on his lap facing him, our breathing turning into kissing.

I look into his face, and there are little oceans in Cory's eyes. He sits against the back wall. His wet eyelashes gather into triangles like stars. "Alley, you can't go now. It's a mess, but we just got moved up to purple today. We can get out of this theater, go someplace decent; we can start making things better."

I shake my head; it doesn't matter.

Cory squeezes my shoulders and the hissing gets intense. "If I could snap my fingers and be mortal, I would. I get it. Being immortal is a trap; it means you never do anything because you can always do it later. There's no urgency, there's no time frame. But I can fight this thing, I can wrestle with The Angel. . . ."

Numb to his promises, I sit silently. He stands up, crosses the room, and gets his smokes from his jacket. "The only reason you stayed with me all these years is because I'm the only one you *could* stay with. Everyone else was going to get old and die on you. You just loved me because you could always come back to me. And now that I don't have that"—he cuts himself off when he sees me staring at him, unmoved— "Alley, what am I going to do when you're gone?"

"You will replace me," I say.

Everything is so quiet I can hear the streetlights change color. My neck is sagging so that I'm staring at the floor. I lift my drooping head with my hands and see Cory craning his neck to look out the circle window.

"I think the Over Workers are here," he says.

"What do they look like?"

"Yuppies."

We both pop our heads out the window, watch the Workers from Over walk down the middle of the empty street. This time around, they come in the form of two men in khaki pants and white, collared shirts, wearing dark sunglasses and carrying briefcases.

We bring our heads back inside. Every weapon or object worth throwing was traded long ago, and as we sit in the attic, unarmed, it's so pathetic and hopeless it's funny.

Cory smiles and says, "Remember that time we ran out of ammunition and threw paper airplanes at them?"

"It was worth a try. We can throw handfuls of cocosmoke butts at them; we've got a lot of those around."

The Workers from Over stop in front of the theater's main entrance, by the ticket booth. There is a pause, and suddenly we hear the rapid fire of gunshots and a woman screaming. It's Kota. Fuck. I forgot she was here. We run down the attic stairs to the box seats overlooking the auditorium. Cory gets ahead as my feet squish into the steps. I can feel my knees start to merge with my calves.

I see Kota with a huge gun in each hand. I call her name.

She looks up, screams, "The bullets are sinking into these fuckers." She must have thought The B&E Boys were back to steal anything she might still own.

"Don't worry about it," I yell. "I think they'll just poop them out later. They're here for me."

Kota's head tilts back to look at me, her gun-toting arms sinking to her sides.

"Alley, these motherfuckers have no eyes," she yells up to the box seats.

"I know. They're blind to the wonder that is."

One of the Workers from Over picks his sunglasses off the floor, and everyone is looking up at us.

"Everybody relax, I'm coming down," I say.

We come down to the auditorium. The Workers from Over stand with briefcases in hand, and Kota is in a stunned haze.

I smile at her. "You thought I was making all this shit up."

She smiles, throws up her hands. She says, "I gotta move these guns and catch a train."

"I'll see you again," I say.

She tilts her head, then nods. "Maybe next life."

"Maybe next life." We hug, and she leaves the theater with her gun trunk. Cory and I face the Over people. If we were going to have a big showdown, now would be the time. Instead I just say to them, "You know, I finally broke the chains of immortality, and I had my own plan for getting out of here. I was even going to cross the ocean and join the revolution. Thanks a fucking lot."

They shrug their shoulders like there's nothing they can do and keep stepping toward me.

"I don't want to go."

They stop. The two identical men look at each other.

"Pardon?" one says.

"I said I don't want to go to Over. Don't you have ears?"

They look at each other. "Would you be willing to fill out some paperwork to that effect?" one says.

"What?" I ask.

"Well, that is the policy."

Now it's Cory's turn. "What?" "If you specifically state that you do not want to accompany us back to Over, you have some options open to you."

"Like what?" I am in shock.

"Like not going back to Over."

"Wow. Uh, sure."

"Excellent. Would you mind if we all had a seat?"

"No, that's fine. We have a million." I am in a daze. We sit across the aisle from the Over Workers in row T, as one man snaps open his briefcase. Cory lights a smoke, his hands shaking. I can't believe I'm sitting down to do paperwork with the people who have been chasing me for a thousand years. I didn't know they had paper. One Over person takes out a flashlight and provides light for the other as he flips through a file.

"Let's begin," the man says, clicking his pen. "Okay, Alison Bojalad. Would you like to return to Over: (A) In a minute. (B) Soon. (C) Later. (D) Much later. (E) Never."

"(E) Never."

He circles it with his pen.

Cory looks at me. "Wouldn't you rather take (D)? Much later?"

"No. I don't want this hanging over my head. No. (E) Never."

"(E) then, very well. Because you have chosen option (E), I am required to read you the following stipulations."

"Spit it out."

He turns the paper and reads from it.

"One: All (E) decisions are final.

"Two: Over will not be sending out any additional staff to collect you. Should you decide to return to Over, you will have to provide your own transportation and discover your own return route.

"Three: Any protection, emotional or physical, once offered by Over is hereby revoked. Over can no longer provide you with an opportunity to be forcibly removed from a place from which you wish to be removed."

Cory and I look at each other.

"Four: Good luck in the world of the living. You're on your own."

He hands over a piece of paper and a pen. "Please sign on the dotted line."

I take a breath, and as I sign it, I feel my body reinflate. I ask, "You're saying in all these years, I never once told you no?"

"Posturing and fighting are commonplace. A real desire to change is quite rare." He takes out a thick slab of paper held together with a big clip. He flips through it. "According to your file, you've taken the following escape routes . . ." He flips pages. "Used the following weapons against Over representatives . . ." Flips more pages. "And used profanity and threats that include the following . . ." He hands over the sections of the packet. "The threat section is alphabetized, so you can see that the phrase 'I don't want to go,' or any reasonable facsimile is not listed, although you demonstrate an extensive range of obscenities."

I give him back the papers. Cory says, "Wait. Do you have a file for me?"

"Your name is?"

"Cory. Cory Carter."

The other representative clicks open his briefcase and takes out a file. "Yes, we have you right here. Would you like to sign a contract as well?"

Cory and I look at each other. He thinks about it, smokes quickly, and bites at his nails.

"No," Cory says finally.

"Would you like to leave a message or schedule an appointment?"

Cory takes a last drag and puts his smoke out in the ashtray in the seat in front of him. Everyone is looking at him. Finally he shakes his head no, never looking up.

"Very well. Thank you and have a good day."

I let them out the door and that's it.

Needless to say, an incredibly awkward silence falls between Cory and me after the door clicks shut. Finally Cory stands up abruptly, angrily.

"Forgive me for being the person I've become," Cory says, walking down the aisle.

"It's the person you've always been!" I yell after him.

Cory wheels around and strides toward me, and his legs are so long that he gets to me in four steps. The gloves are off.

"You're a junkie. Just like me, Alison," he yells. "You blame me! You blame me for all of this, like you're some princess. Well, you know what, Alison, you're gonna take yourself with you wherever you go. Mark my words on this one: anyplace you go will become Neom, and any guy you love is going to turn into me. So you come and find me after ten men, ten cities, and ten years—and you tell me if anything has changed! Besides you being older."

He looks for something to throw, but all the chairs are secured to the floor. He waves his finger at me. "And getting older does not mean getting smarter. Just because time passes, it doesn't mean things change. If we've learned one fucking thing in all these years, we've learned that."

"What am I supposed to fucking do, Cory? Stay here and get killed by Atom if he escaped before the explosion? It's not Atom who fucked me up. Atom just does the things that bad guys and kingpins and moneylenders do. It's his nature. But you are my husband, and you were supposed to be something righteous. Something loyal. So maybe I'll go somewhere else and be a fuckup, but maybe I've gotten strong. You know? You have no idea. I'm not scared of the blue monsters on the map anymore, and I can find my way. You have no idea what I'm capable of."

He turns around and goes toward the door.

"I am stronger than you know!" I yell after him.

Now what do I do?

I get lit and go to the Easy Store to buy soap.

When I return, I hear someone shuffling around in the attic. It doesn't sound like Cory. I stop at the bottom of the attic stairs.

"Hello?" I say.

"What?" It is a girl's voice. I go up the stairs, and Dilly Dally is standing there. The attic looks different; she's already lit candles and started rearranging the mats.

"Why the hell are you here?" I ask.

"Why the hell are *you* here? This isn't your place anymore."

Cripes, that was fast.

"Go to hell," I say and start up the stairs. I snag my satchel. I tip over the stop sign that's on top of the box and open the lid. I take a few things and grab the map The Bandits gave me, the one that shows where they're going, and where to find them. Running off with The Bandits might be a bad choice, but it's *my* choice, the first choice in a life that now belongs to me.

"Where's the notebook that was on the table?"

"What notebook?"

"The only goddamn book in this attic, you idiot. It's called *Anatomy of an Oval* and it was here."

"Oh, it's gone," she says lightly. "Cory took it to sell it."

And then she smiles. I am about to kill her, when I notice a bunch of sandbags she's brought up from the stage area, the counterweights.

Dilly Dally sees me looking at the weights. She tries to block my view and distract me by telling me I should leave, I've been replaced, blah blah blah. One candle flickers and her shadow jiggles out of step.

She's too late. I figured it out.

"Dilly," I say slowly and clearly. "Where's Ray?"

Her eyes dart around as she grasps for a lie. "I don't know who you're talking about," she says.

"Oh yes you do. You are the one person who's going to remember Ray. Because you and Ray are the same kind of . . . fragment . . . splinter . . . ghost thing. Ray splintered off Cory and you splintered off me, and now you've got sandbags set up all over the place because you're scared your shadows are going to grab you and make you float away, too."

Her jaw is visibly clenching.

I smile and start teasing her, "Hey, Dilly, your shadow's moving; it's gonna come getcha. Better go put that sandbag on top of it to weigh it down."

She glares at me and growls, spins around and heaves a sandbag on top of a shadow that's coming at her with a dark, translucent net.

"Cory can have you, Dilly. You're just the shadow I leave behind, some dope who can tolerate being his chain. I just hope I'm splintering off the pathetic part of myself that needs to be rescued."

Her eyes fill with tears.

"And the part of me that cries a lot."

I shake my head in disgust, leave the attic, and go behind the stage, open the fake wall, and steal all of Cory's mugs. I paid for them with my soul, and it's time to cash out. It's not like Cory will starve; he'll get fronted a few new shipments and that will make up for the loss—or he'll trade Dilly. Whatever.

Luckily, there's still an underground of the underground. May Daisy still has her network of chains who skim and sell to normal people in the downtown area. I keep as much inventory as I can comfortably carry and sell the rest to her. I don't explain where it came from or tell her I'm leaving.

I walk away from the park and find myself on the corner of a busy street. Cars are whizzing by, and people are walking around, very busy at what they're doing. It's a warm, beautiful day. I take off the heavy shirt I was wearing over my dress and tie it around my waist, thinking that the world suddenly seems like a very strange place. Here I am, trying to make a bold escape, but I've been dumped and have to shuffle out. I even had a plan to protect myself from Cory's voodoo love magic when he came after me, trying to get me back. It seems funny now, thinking about my plan to stay strong by imagining myself stepping into the blue waters of the unknown; a vision that would keep me from falling under his spell. I shake my head and smile at the thought. I sit on a stone bench and take The Bandits' map out of my pocket and look at it closely, look at the train stop that connects to the speed train for the ferry. I'll find The Bandits there and cross the river to a bigger boat that travels to Capital City. The blue water section of the map has a picture of a creature that looks like a dinosaur, with a big open mouth and sharp teeth and a stinger on his tail. I've seen worse.

I head for the train station that will take me to the meeting place. As I walk, I imagine myself in an amplified life, one where Geisai Clubs serve as the backdrop for the secret Army of the Revolution, and power swirls in the air of Capital City. It sounds good to me.

I wonder what we're revolting against.

I run down the cement steps to the underground train just as the doors shut tight and the train rumbles away. Time to wait.

Suddenly I start to get a very anxious feeling. I look down the tube and see nothing. Then I hear footsteps and see Cory's tired brown shoes coming down the steps.

Shit.

Cory's old necklace is gone, and a new, blue-purple stone has replaced it. He doesn't seem angry anymore, just says, "Hey, Alley, how's it going?"

I nervously say, "Okay."

He says, "Heading off?"

"Yes," I say. "I stole your stash."

He nods and pulls a box of smokes out of his front pocket. "I gathered as much."

"I'm sorry."

"Well, I'm sorry, too. Sorry about a number of things."

I take off my wedding bracelet and offer it to him. "This should be worth something."

Cory just looks at it. "Yes, I would hope that our marriage is worth something."

I look at the only person I've ever loved in my whole life. A thousand years of history swirl around us, and a love for him starts coursing through my blood like a disease that turns you into a zombie.

The underground begins to rumble.

"You don't have to go," Cory says.

"Yes, I do."

"No, you don't." He hands me a tiny bottle of Drinkme, one of the culprits of Mushy Brain Syndrome, but a powerful amnesiac that wipes out the past. He says, "The train makes a huge loop, the entire circumference of Neom. If you drink that, by the time you come around, you'll have forgotten everything, and you'll see the good side of me again; it will feel like Ray has returned. We'll start over, we'll start new, we'll make new promises. I'll show you around the theater, show you the stars; we'll act like we've never seen it before."

He moves in closer. "We'll stand on a mountain and burn down every fucker who's ever done us wrong. You won't be alone in your revenge."

I'm slowly shaking my head, feeling like I've already drunk from the bottle. I visualize sailing away on the blue water as Cory tucks the bottle into my satchel. He strokes my hair, holds my face in his hands.

"Just get on the train and drink the bottle while you circle the city. Don't get off at any stop, just stay put, and when it comes back around, I'll be here, waiting. I'll give back your wedding bracelet and"—he kisses my forehead and whispers—"I promise you, next time around, things will be different."

The train comes and I step on, turning to face Cory. The doors close between us, and I wave good-bye.

# ACKNOWLEDGMENTS

Very sincere thanks go out to the folks who supported the very early drafts, which were written long ago. To Rima Merriman and the Individualized Major Program at Indiana University, who arranged for a generous amount of support from such writers as Maura Stanton, John W. Johnson, and Yusef Komunyakaa. A thank you also to those from back in the day: Amy Flack, Amy Reese, Joe, Kaia Roewade, Adam Bruce, Thomasina, Matt Flowermonster, Kristine Kelly, Blaize, Randy, Kimball, Matty Dee, Forest Greenleaf Gras, Heather Leffler, Pam MacLaughlin, Malik Turley, Eve, Asha Greer, Cory Carter, Ray, Zeke, Tom Kowal, and the Rainbow Family. But most of all, I thank Professor Ardizzone, without whom this novel would never have been written, and I might not have made it all the way here.

Thank you also to Mark Heineke, for giving me total artistic freedom and publishing an artistically uncompromised novel. Thank you to Zhanna Vaynberg for the great final edit, and thank you to a long list of additional people to whom I owe a debt of gratitude: among them are Alex Schwartz, Joanna Topor MacKenzie, Mick Nan, Rachel Posner, Audrey Mast, and Terri Griffith. I also want to thank the dozens of readers on CritiqueCircle.com who helped me as I updated and finished this novel.

My love to my family, my best friend (still), Amy, and my husband, Dan.